THE ONLY GOOD APPLE
IN A BARREL OF SPIES

THE ONLY GOOD APPLE
IN A BARREL OF SPIES

MARC LOVELL

PUBLISHED FOR THE CRIME CLUB BY

DOUBLEDAY & COMPANY, INC.

GARDEN CITY, NEW YORK

1984

All of the characters in this book
are fictitious, and any resemblance
to actual persons, living or dead,
is purely coincidental.

Library of Congress Cataloging in Publication Data

Lovell, Marc.
The only good apple in a barrel of spies.

I. Title.
PR6062.0853055   1984   823'.914
ISBN:0-385-19457-9

Library of Congress Catalog Card Number 84-4107
Copyright © 1984 by Doubleday & Company, Inc.
All Rights Reserved
Printed in the United States of America
First Edition

THE ONLY GOOD APPLE
IN A BARREL OF SPIES

ONE

It was a dark and stormy night.

Wind whooped or pleaded around the cottage like a battle between the civilised and the primitive. Minor debris blown up from the lane tapped erratically, eerily on the bow-window. The ceiling beams creaked and a door upstairs rattled. Once in a while, a shower of rain passed by as if to say "Shush" to all the others.

Apple loved it. This weekend he had felt particularly cosy and secure in his country retreat, which seemed a whole continent away from the Bloomsbury flat, not a mere forty-five-minute drive. He was glad that autumn had arrived.

Bullied along by a fresh gust of wind, leaves and twigs clattered urgently on the curtained window. The sound broke Apple's concentration. He lowered the book he was reading.

With a smile he looked around—at the firelight dancing on the old walls, at the chintz and brassware, at the blazing logs, at his dog stretched out asleep on the hearth-rug. A standard lamp beside his rocking-chair created deep shadows on his face.

Appleton Porter's face was pleasant, unremarkable on first glance, and still so on second except perhaps for the green eyes with their vague hint of apprehension. Across his nose and pale cheeks lay a sprinkling of freckles. His hair, ginger-fair, was cut neatly short.

Apple had a tall, tall body that was slim but not skinny. Tomorrow, Monday, it would be back in the drab, hated business suit; since Friday night it had luxuriated in its present gumboots, mud-spattered corduroys and ancient sweater.

Apple despaired of his unusual height as strongly as he disliked his looks. He had no illusions about himself, only a few delusions about life in general.

As an expression of his comfort, Apple began to move his rocking-chair gently. The faint squeak of wood was noted by Monico, who had been deaf to all the other noises of the night, and who now lifted his head from the rug.

Apple leaned forward. "No, I'm not getting up," he said. "We're not going for a walk. Sorry. But I don't think you have cause for complaint about exercise."

Monico gazed up at him stonily.

Apple said, "Furthermore, we both have to be up early in the morning. No lazy lie-ins. I have to return you to Galling's farm before I set off for . . ."

He didn't bother to finish the explanation: Monico, a long-legged Ibizan hound, had closed his eyes and dropped his head back to the rug—possibly, Apple mused, at mention of the place where he boarded during the week, which he didn't like, being nervous of the stock and poultry.

"It's not my fault," Apple said. "*I* didn't make the no-pets rule in Harlequin Mansions."

Monico merely twitching his toes, pretending to be asleep and dreaming, Apple gave up, after a repeat of "It's not my fault." They had been through all this before.

Still gently rocking, Apple began again to read. The book, a recent publication, was a spy story. Apple bought every new spy novel that came out. He also saw every

movie with an espionage theme and watched any television production that was of the same type. If, however,
the printed or pictorial offering was non-fiction, he allowed it to escape his notice. That the spy game was
romantic and glamorous rather than cold and grubby was
one of Apple's more coveted delusions.

He quickly became engrossed in the novel.

Its hero was tough, handsome, skilled and of average
height. He was so much in demand, yet so indifferent to
his success, that his Control often had either to plead or
use blackmail to get him to take on a mission. Women fell
passionately in love with him every time he lit a cigarette.

Apple read in the deepest concentration. His envy
stood at a discreet distance. It stayed there until two of the
hero's colleagues started to discuss him out of his hearing.
They spoke of the star agent with such respect, near awe,
that Apple's eyes grew red.

Sighing, he let the book sag to his lap. He stared into
the fire. Of its own accord, his imagination produced a
scene similar to the one he had just been reading. That the
pair of agents in the duologue were vague of face was
because Apple knew few of his colleagues in British Intelligence; that he changed the locale from a Moscow tavern
to a London inn was because he had never been to Russia.
Apple did not have a strong imagination.

The first man said, "Hard as iron, that Appleton Porter."

"Brave as well."

"True. He has nerves of steel."

The second man said, "And he can drink the old fire-
water for hours without turning a hair."

"Angus Watkin uses him every chance he gets."

"One of your real tough, ruthless professionals, that's
what Porter is."

Apple cringed inside at the outrageous quality of the lies. However, instead of leaving the reverie, which he was enjoying, for it was the closest he had been to the spy business in months, he switched over to the truth.

The first man asked, "You knew that Porter was a linguist, didn't you?"

"Of course. He speaks seven languages fluently, without a trace of an accent."

"He also has a good knowledge of about a dozen others."

The second man said, "He's done some great desk work as an interpreter at peak conferences between NATO spook-chiefs, as well as translating all kinds of information."

"Right."

"Right."

Both men, who were sitting at a table over beers, nodded firmly and quickly. The nods slowed, became less firm, and then stopped. There was a pause—Apple blinking sadly—before the first man said, "He's a faceless one. You know the type."

"Sure. Forger, hypnotist, cat burglar or, as in his case, language freak, these oddball specialists rarely get used by Upstairs, sent out into the field."

"In Appleton Porter's case it's understandable—apart from his interpreting jobs. To begin with, he's six feet seven inches tall."

The other man shook his head sympathetically. "Christ, the poor bastard."

"He'd have a hard time merging that beanpole body with a crowd of normal people."

"And did you know he was soft-hearted?"

"Yes, I did," the first agent said. "Not only that, but he

has this fetish of collecting useless bits of data. He's an infomaniac."

"Still, maybe his training scores were high."

"Dismal, old man. Believe me. I've seen his dossier. After languages and security clearance, 10 each, he scores low in almost everything: unarmed combat, tolerance for alcohol, lying ability, pain endurance, you name it."

The other man shook his head again. "Poor old Russet."

The first agent shook his head also. "Who?"

"You didn't know Porter's nickname? They call him Russet after that type of apple."

"Why's that?"

The scene shimmered as Apple protested, but strengthened again as he decided to forge ahead. Apple could be cruel—when the victim was himself.

The other agent said, "It's because he has this awful habit of blushing."

"You must be putting me on."

Apple had had enough. He ended the scene there. It was part cowardice, part the fact that he could feel a blush working its way up from his chest. He would now need his imagination to make another, different picture.

The latest in Apple's short-term cures for his affliction he had been given by a fellow-sufferer, not, as customary, bought by way of an advertisement in a magazine. Like the others, however, it was based on the concepts of heat and fear—the former to overwhelm the facial warmth, the latter to belittle causation.

Apple visualised a vast cavern (poached from illustrations of Dante's Inferno). It was acrawl with wailing sinners and shrieking devils (the noise from outside helped). By means of a pulley connected with the roof, a demon was lowering Apple towards a cauldron of boiling oil (his mild rocking in the chair aided the illusion). Only inches now separated his feet from the scorching turbulence (he had edged his gumboots closer to the log fire).

Assisted by those externals, plus the fact of being alone, Apple won a quick victory. The blush never quite reached his face. Easing to a halt at the jawline, it crept back down to whence it came.

Cool and relieved, Apple picked up his book. After skipping pages to cut out the eulogising duologue, he once more settled to reading. He turned back into the hero.

Thirty minutes later Monico jerked his head up. Apple leaned forward and met his dog's eyes, which then swivelled to one side, aimed in the direction of the little-used lane outside. His ears twitched.

As far as Apple was concerned, there was nothing different to be heard from outdoors; but he knew that canine hearing was 120 per cent better than the human variety, therefore he waited and listened.

It was, however, the visual which got to him first. The bow-window's curtains silvered as they were hit by the headlights of a car. That gone, the sound of a motor grew. It stopped and died on coming level with the cottage.

Apple got up. After dropping his book on the chair, he went to the door, which was a solid slab of wood. He supposed that outside he would find a lost Sunday excursionist, behind which thought he was hoping for a maiden in distress (flat tyre, dry petrol tank, whatever); a beautiful girl who would come into his life from out of the storm. And this time it would be the real thing.

Apple unbolted the door. He opened it far enough to get his head through the space. Wind tossed his hair about like grass on a hilltop.

Peering through the dimness created by light seeping past the curtains, Apple saw the car. It was black and of medium age and size.

The sole occupant got out, came forward. The figure was neither female nor beautiful. Nevertheless, Apple felt a flush of excitement as he watched the man who strolled along the garden path.

He was small, wiry, middle-aged and with white hair. His features, coarse as a workman's glove, were like those of someone who didn't get enough sleep out of self-spite. He wore a soiled blue boiler suit and running shoes that had once been white.

"Good evening, Albert," Apple said, playing it cool to the point of indifference.

Albert said, "Well, well, if it isn't the tallest dwarf in the world." His accent was cockney.

Apple answered with merely a pale smile. He didn't like the jibe but was restrained by his knowledge that the older man, despite looking a wreck, was a genius at every known system of unarmed combat, as well as some of his own invention.

Albert asked, "Or are you the smallest giant?"

Hoping that his excitement wasn't showing, Apple said mildly, "Your wit is as original as ever. Come in."

"Thought you'd never ask."

Apple stood back. Closing the door against the wind when the visitor had entered, he said, "Don't worry about the dog. He never attacks anyone."

Albert looked both disappointed and disapproving. He said it was all a matter of diet. "Try feeding the poor ugly thing on raw meat."

Apple increased his height by a quarter inch. "May I enquire the nature of your brief call?"

The reply was an accusation. "You haven't got a blower."

"I have never felt the need here for a telephone."

"Then you're mad. This is the back of bloody beyond. I never would've found you if it hadn't been for that ice-cream cart outside."

"If you're referring to my car," Apple said, admiring his self-control. "Well, never mind." In moving away from the threshold, he saw his novel lying face-up on the rocking chair. He quickened his step.

"Don't bother to offer me a drink or anything," Albert said in a tone as subtle as forked lightning. "I don't have the time to spare."

Apple picked up his novel and put it on the mantelshelf. "We're out of everything."

"And you needn't bother to offer me that book either. I've read it."

"It's a translation job I have to do."

"Good plot, I thought."

"Really?"

"The Red agent everyone's looking for, he turns out to be the British Ambassador."

Lethally, Apple said, "Thank you."

Albert smiled. "One tries to inform, as the boss always says."

The boss was Apple's Control, Angus Watkin, whom the man known as Albert served as a combination butler, driver, bodyguard and messenger-boy. Which reminder drew Apple away from his annoyance and back to his excitement.

He said, "I take it you have a message for me."

The older man, still on the threshold, shook his head. "No, I haven't."

Apple said, "Oh." Monico gave a faint whine.

"What I got for you's an order," Albert said. "From Mr. Watkin. He wants to see you."

Brightening, Apple nodded. "Yes, of course. He wants to see me tomorrow morning, I imagine." He added, as a temptation to luck, "As early as possible, no doubt."

Albert again shook his head. "No."

"Mid-morning?"

"No."

"Noon?"

"Nor that."

"How about tea-time?"

The man in the boiler suit said, "Mr. Watkin wants to see you now."

Apple blinked slowly three times. "Now? The chief's here, in the car?"

Albert put on an expression of scorn. "What, Mr. Watkin wait in a car for the likes of you?"

"Of course not. Silly of me."

"He's in a pub in the village back there."

Apple's excitement flared like a dancer's red skirt. He had expected to receive a summons to attend on the great man in London. That would have been good enough. But for Angus Watkin to come almost to the underling's doorstep, give or take a mile, that was startlingly unusual and of day-dream quality.

However, Apple acted the efficient operative in saying, "Very well, Albert. It'll take me ten minutes to change."

The older man turned to the door and drew it open. *"Now* is what I said." He went out. "Follow me in your ice-cream cart, Antonio."

Seconds later, Apple, buffeted by the wind, was opening the rear door of Ethel for his dog to get in. Ethel was an ancient London taxi. Apple had acquired her after her retirement from government service, which had included many years in undercover work with Intelligence.

The high, square vehicle's traditional black had been
replaced with a brightness that Apple would never dare
don himself, though he longed to. When in his car, he just
as much wore it as drove it.

Mainly, Ethel was pale green. To that was added an
orange stripe around her middle and wheels of brash red.
She was a dowager on a capricious spree.

Moving off with the black car in his headlights, Apple
smiled. He had Ethel, he had Monico, and there was probably adventure ahead.

The village, one straggly main street with dim lamps,
was void of movement except for two sheets of newspaper; windblown, they cavorted along gleefully like young
phantoms just let out of haunting class.

The pub, Ye Weary Traveller, had a mock-Tudor
façade and signs made of wrought iron. Like Apple's cottage, it was old but pretending to be archaic.

The car in front began to slow. It came to a stop
opposite the pub. After its rear lights had winked four
times, the black car went on again.

Apple sighed at the overdone office-giving. He wasn't
sure if Albert thought him dim-witted or was getting in
yet another dig at his amateur status.

However, Apple declined to be annoyed or depressed. He was too stimulated, too full of the possibilities
which had occurred to him relating to the imminent operation. They ranged from a parachute drop behind the
Iron Curtain to chasing a traitor in Turkey.

The black car had gone from sight around a bend by
the time Apple had parked in the kerb. He didn't bother
to lock Ethel. Anyone bent on theft would, in his inno-
cence, be scared off by Monico.

Reminding himself of various single, multi-meaning

verbs in Turkish, such as "to be impossible to be made to be hated," Apple went into Ye Weary Traveller.

There was one large room, with a scattering of iron pillars to support the ceiling, which had regular sags. Late now, the place was packed. Some 10 per cent of those present were smartly dressed; they were locals. The rest, weekenders from the city, played countryfolk in various forms of bucolic garb, including the odd straw hat.

Being known here, Apple drew no special attention as he made his way over to the corner table. He noticed that the man who sat there, though neither weekender nor local, still managed to blend.

Angus Watkin looked unnecessary. He was like that man they used as background material in motion picture scenes: so void of colour that there was no risk of him drawing attention away from the main players.

Angus Watkin was middle-aged, middle-height, middle-weight, middle-neat. The dull eyes in his middle-type face appeared to express sensibleness rather than intelligence. His fawn raincoat was buttoned to the neck, as though to say Keep Out, Danger of Boredom.

Stopping at the table, Apple bent politely and said, "Good evening, sir."

Angus Watkin nodded a greeting. His eyes swept lazily up and down Apple's clothes with a hint of distaste. He said, "Be seated, Porter."

While sitting, Apple noted that, as expected, his chief had ordered him his favourite drink, sherry on the rocks. He said, "Thank you, sir."

"Thank Accounts," Watkin said in his drab voice. "This is their treat." He lifted his glass as though it contained medicine, not, as Apple knew, Scotch and water, sipped once and accused, "You have no telephone."

"That's true."

"Get one."

"Yes, sir," Apple said, his excitement merry.

After another sip Angus Watkin put his drink down. "I have a job for you."

Apple's feelings paused. Whereas in spookspeak "little errand" meant a full-scale espionage mission, "job" meant playing a minor role in someone else's operation, some five-minute or half-hour task such as dropping a paperback book, or pretending to use a public telephone to prevent it being used by an enemy at a particular time.

"But it's urgent?" Apple asked.

"No, Porter. Your job is tomorrow. I came out here to the wilds because I enjoy a Sunday outing."

The only thing you enjoy, Apple thought sourly, is the power you have over your underlings.

"Tomorrow at noon, Porter. You should be able to fit this job in during the lunch break from that place at which you work." He made the United Kingdom Philological Institute sound like a rag-picker's hovel. "All right?"

"Of course, sir."

"Good," Angus Watkin said. "You may smoke, if you can't manage without."

While lighting up, Apple told himself that any kind of involvement was better than none at all. In his position, well below the bottom step of those that led to Upstairs, he had to be grateful for any crumb that came his way.

"Ready to absorb, Porter?"

"Ready, sir."

"Four days ago," Angus Watkin said, "at three-thirty in the afternoon, a man died on a platform of the London underground railway system. His name was Narkov. Possibly you read a brief press report of the event."

Apple nodded. "I did, yes. He was the cultural attaché at the Red Shed."

"The Soviet Embassy," Watkin murmured. He disapproved of trade cant. "By design, some of my people were present. They took charge of matters so were able to give the body and its effects a thorough going over before turning the late attaché over to his countrymen."

"That was lucky, sir."

"Luck had no bearing on it, Porter. Please pay closer attention."

"Sorry, sir."

Angus Watkin said, "Death, it seemed, was due to a cardiac seizure. Narkov had been in extremely bad health. He lived on a strict diet, and his wife made very sure that he followed it to the letter. In other words, we fully accept that Narkov died of natural causes."

Apple said, "I see, sir."

"I'm sure that you do not," Watkin said. "But it doesn't matter. Cheers."

"Cheers."

While they sipped their drinks, Apple had a glance around. As before, the people at neighbouring tables were busy with their own talk.

Swirling the contents of his glass, Angus Watkin said, "There was nothing of interest to me in Narkov's pockets, and nothing hidden in his clothing. The body, in fact, was as straightforward as the cause of its demise."

Apple was happy to flatter with, "In that case, sir, I don't understand."

"Why the continuing interest? Quite."

"Perhaps you feel the search wasn't thorough enough."

"No, Porter, I have faith in my people. The point is, the whole thing jarred. To begin with, Narkov was on the southbound platform of the Bakerloo Line, at Piccadilly Circus."

"And if he was heading for home," Apple said, "he ought to have been northbound, so he could change to the Central Line at Oxford Circus."

Ignoring the interruption, Angus Watkin said, "In the second place, Narkov's actions had been somewhat odd in the weeks previous to his death. That, I might add, is an understatement." He sniffed. "Are you going to smoke that thing down to the filter?"

Muttering an apology, Apple stubbed out his cigarette, even though it had been smoked only midway.

Watkin said, "Lastly, our cultural attaché was *not* a member of or an employee of the KGB."

Both to toady and to redeem himself, Apple asked, although knowing the answer, "Isn't that unusual, sir?" His Control loved to enlighten.

"It is, Porter. The average here and elsewhere is for one third of Soviet Embassy staff to be involved in unauthorised activities, and for all those bearing titles, as did Narkov. Unusual indeed."

Angus Watkin again swirled the remains of his Scotch and water, as if, Apple thought, it were an expensive brandy. He drank, put down the empty glass and said, "However, there was nothing we could do about the Narkov business, not until a couple of days ago. A new face showed up on the scene."

"Which scene is it, sir?"

"That, Porter, you will learn in due course, along with a word or two on what your job entails."

Apple cleared his throat raspily, irked with himself for forgetting need-to-know: information in sequence.

"The new face belongs to a woman," Angus Watkin said. "She, I am happy to say, also jars, for several reasons. Possibly, there is no connection whatever with the late

Russian gentleman, but . . ." He wound up the sentence with a gesture.

"Exactly, sir. No stone unturned."

"And that, Porter, is all I have to tell you, and I had no real need to tell you that much. I'm in an expansive mood this evening."

Apple's surprise at the last statement, the closest his chief had ever come to seeming human, cut into his disappointment at not being about to hear more on the mystery woman.

After taking a lazy look at his watch, Watkin said, "You will present yourself at 47 Regent Street, Suite 9, tomorrow at twelve sharp."

"Yes, sir," Apple said, adding aloud a repeat of the place and time. He straightened his back. "And thank you for giving me this opportunity."

Beginning to rise from his seat, Angus Watkin said happily, enigmatically, "You are the tallest man I've got."

Next morning, Apple got up at seven o'clock. He bustled as he went about his tasks of tidying, showering, dressing in the dull suit he wore to the office, fixing breakfast for himself and Monico.

Although he had gone to sleep with mixed emotions over his job for Watkin, Apple had awoken to a return of his excitement, though it was in a milder form.

And quite right too, he thought as he reached for the frying-pan. Half a crust was better than no bread; his height, it appeared, was actually doing him some good; and there was a chance of seeing a woman who might be involved in some high-up espionage caper.

After breakfast (a bacon sandwich apiece), Apple took Monico across fields behind the cottage. The storm had died with the darkness, but autumn's bite was still in the air.

Within five minutes of leaving his dog with farmer Galling, Apple was heading for London, sitting at the steering-wheel of Ethel, who was only part responsible this morning for her owner's quiet smile.

Apple wondered about the relationship between his height and the job. Did he have to play a shopkeeper, and reach to a high shelf? Did he have to check on someone's reading matter by looking over his shoulder? Did he have to pass on some sort of message above the heads of a crowd?

The more Apple thought about it, the more possibilities occurred to him. He was titillated, as well as uplifted, by there being so many advantages to tallness. He drove as swiftly as Ethel's great age would allow.

In Kensington, Apple parked and went into the imposing building which housed the United Kingdom Philological Institute. Being here a senior official, despite the comparative youth of his twenty-eight years, Apple was entitled to arrive late and leave early. He rarely did either.

In his poky office on an upper floor, Apple tried to settle to his current work—a lecture he was composing on the near-defunct Manx language. He found himself unable to concentrate.

Not for the first time, Apple wished he had someone in whom he could confide. But no one at the institute, not even its principal, Professor Warden, knew of his connection with British Intelligence. Come to that, Apple mused despondently while doodling a parachute, nobody else knew either, outside of a handful of Upstairs people.

Sighing, Apple once again tried to work. If he didn't, the morning would be endless, he knew. This time he succeeded, though he wouldn't have if the task had been related to anything other than his intellectual passion—language.

Manx, of the Goidelic branch of Celtic, kept Apple busy until shortly after eleven o'clock, at which time his emotional passion began to interrupt.

Sliding his half-finished composition into a drawer, he left his office, went downstairs and out to the street. His guilt, for quitting before due time, he enjoyed on a subversive level. That was something else he had been looking forward to during the morning.

With time to spare, Apple set off to walk to the West End. He marched with his arms swinging and his excitement at a pleasant simmer.

It was twelve o'clock minus one minute when Apple entered a doorway on Regent Street; twelve precisely when he passed through the second-floor door which said Trident Imports, Reception, Please Enter.

The room had bare walls, linoleum flooring, a dozen or so upright chairs and one occupant. As Apple closed the door behind him, the man got up to come forward.

He was in his late thirties, bald and stout. His bow-tie and yellow shoes and suit of loud stripes were matched by a pink, brash, cheerful face. He looked as if he had just won a prize for sartorial daring. He made Apple feel like offering an apology.

"We'll call each other Ned," the man said briskly as he gave Apple's hand a perfunctory shake. "That's best." He tapped Apple on the chest. "Okay with you, Ned?"

"Yes, Ned, of course."

The man afted his hands as he took a step backwards. He said, "Right you are. So let's get on with it. Show me your wallet, if you please."

Knowing the oddness of the spy game, Apple didn't

hesitate. He reached into his inside breast pocket. Except for a comb, it was empty.

He frowned. "That's funny. I could've sworn . . ."

"Here it is," Ned said. From behind his back he brought his hands. In one of them was the missing wallet. "Sorry about that, Ned."

Impressed, Apple said, "No need to be, Ned. It was a brilliant bit of work."

"Thanks. Dipping happens to be my specialty. Yours, I reckon, is being on the tall side."

"Mmm," Apple non-committed. He was aware of voices from behind an interior door.

Ned rubbed the wallet on his loud sleeve. "Nice bit of leather, this," he said. He came forward. "If you close your eyes and count to one, Ned, I'll put it back."

Apple obliged. He felt only the slightest of movements. "Congratulations."

"I just happen to be a genius at the dipping lark, that's all there is to it."

"Even so."

"But let's get on, Ned," Ned said, still brisk. "See, I've got to tell you how to be the reverse—a victim."

"Really?" Apple said—lightly, even though he didn't like the sound of it.

"First of all, you've got to look rich. The way to do that is to stare around you as if you're not happy to be among a mob of proletarians. It's just not what you're used to, this kind of travel."

"What kind, Ned?"

"Underground train. We're going to Piccadilly Station in a minute."

"And I'm going to be your victim?"

"No, Ned," Ned said patiently. "Someone else's. Now listen. As well as looking rich, the other thing you've got to do is touch the outside of your pocket the moment you see a beware-of-pickpockets sign."

Apple said, "If there is one."

"There's always one in stations and suchlike places. If the authorities haven't put one up, or if an old one's faded or been damaged, the dip puts one up himself."

Apple raised his eyebrows. "Pickpockets post warnings against themselves?"

Ned nodded happily. It wasn't often, Apple supposed, that he got a chance to talk shop. "Some have 'em printed, some just scrawl the message in chalk. Actually, that one's often best. Has a look of freshness, see, as if the danger's just arrived."

"But why do they do it?"

"Because when people who're carrying cash or whatever see a sign, they automatically touch where the goods're sitting. It's instinct. And that's what the dips watch for."

"I follow," Apple said. "It's neat."

"Rarely fails, Ned," Ned said.

"Yet you just told me to be sure to touch my pocket when I see a sign."

"Well, your training might hold you in check, see."

"I'll make sure it doesn't."

"Right," Ned said. "That leaves us with only one problem. She might not dip you."

"She? Who?"

"A female called Sylvia. At least, that's the code-name she's been given."

Ah, the woman in the case, Apple thought. He asked, "What's she like?"

"Young. Under twenty-five, I'd say. Good to look at. A bit of a mystery."

"Well now. That's very interesting."

"It won't be if she doesn't dip you."

"I get the picture," Apple said. "We want to find out if this girl's a pickpocket."

Ned shook his head. "She represents herself to be that already. No, Ned, we want her to pick your pocket for two reasons. First, to see if she's genuine, a real pro."

"And the best way to do that," Apple said, feeling clever, "is to see if she can dip the inside breast pocket of a rather tall man."

Ned looked at him with approval. "Good for you, Ned."

"So what's the second reason?"

"That's none of my business," Ned said. "Let's go."

Who is Sylvia, what is she?

The refrain ran through Apple's head as he went down the stairs with the dipping genius. He was immensely titillated by the girl who had been so suitably code-named. She was young, she was good to look at, she was a mystery.

A mystery in all ways to Ned, apparently, Apple mused; otherwise he would have made a reference to some possible connection with the dead cultural attaché. It was standard, all part of need-to-know.

Apple and Ned, coming out onto Regent Street, began to walk towards Piccadilly Circus. In every way from build to clothing they were as well matched as fish and honey.

Apple said, "Haven't the police shown an interest in our girl Sylvia?" He had been going to ask why Angus Watkin hadn't had Scotland Yard question the girl, but had realised that that, of course, might frighten Sylvia off.

"Coppers in the West End gave up on pickpockets long ago," Ned said. "It's like shop-lifting. The shop itself has to do the prosecuting, the coppers won't. There's too much of both nowadays."

"What if someone were to complain to a policeman that his pocket had been picked?"

"The bobby'd give the poor sod a smile—of sympathy or scorn, depending like."

Apple grunted and went back to thinking about young mysteries who were good to look at.

A moment later he and Ned were going down the steps to the underground station. People moved by thickly in both directions. Wind came gusting up from below, making everyone look to be in a panic.

Out of daylight, into artificial lighting, Apple followed Ned onto the concourse. It was circular, like the Circus above. Around the low sides, between posters and the station's offices, were cramped businesses: heel bars, news-stands, confectionary counters. It was like an Eastern bazaar dressed in glazed tile. The jabber of the thronging noontimers helped.

Over his shoulder Ned said, "Hold on here for a bit, Ned. I'll do a tour to locate Sylvia."

"How do you know she's here?"

"Because I was told. Now don't go away."

"I won't."

"Act natural. Act as if you're waiting for somebody."

"I am," Apple said. "You."

"Right," Ned said, moving on. "Ta-ta, Ned."

Apple moved over to the outer wall, where he stood with his back to a poster that was extolling a new washing powder. After a show of glancing at his watch, he gazed around while wearing a waiting expression. He also sagged at the knees slightly so as not to attract casual attention, thus reducing himself to a mere six feet four.

Ned was back almost at once, to Apple's disappointment; he had just started to feel that he was getting that waiting expression right.

Ned said, "Past that bank of ticket machines. Fair hair, blue suit, white gloves, altogether a bit of all right. Off you go, Ned. Good losing."

Apple moved off with a pro, casual, "See you." He would have stayed in the sag except for remembering that his height was of the essence on this job.

He also remembered his expression. He changed it, trying to match thoughts of richness and Rolls-Royces and luxury accommodation.

Catching sight of himself in a section of mirror, Apple felt a little unnerved. He didn't know whether he looked sinister or ill. Nevertheless he persevered with the expression of cold disdain.

Beyond the ticket machines, Apple saw the girl who had to be Sylvia. She stood among other people near a wall-pasted sign that said Beware of Pickpockets.

Average height, shapely of build, Sylvia had shoulder-length light brown hair and a pretty face. Her eyes were the same colour as the neat suit. With her gloves and a shopping basket, she looked like that nice girl from the suburbs who doesn't really exist anymore.

Apple moved in Sylvia's direction. In case she glanced his way, which is what he wanted her to do, he kept his eyes off her face, seeing her mistily from various edges of his direct vision.

When close, Apple looked up at the warning sign. With a snap, he changed his expression from disdain to alarm. He was surprised to realise that, even before his mind had given the order, his left hand was rising towards the right side of his chest.

Continuing that movement, he patted the lump

there. Then, again quickly, he dropped the hand, glanced all around and switched his features to blankness.

Apple passed slowly with the crowd in front of where Sylvia was standing.

Nothing happened.

Feeling dull and useless, Apple kept going. He wanted to look back, but told himself that wasn't a good idea. Sylvia might, in fact, be following, to catch him unawares. Apple brightened.

He stopped by a news-stand. One minute he spent in perusing the lurid covers of paperback novels. Turning, he saw that Sylvia was still in the same place. He headed back.

This time, Apple strolled with hands afted. Not really knowing how to look rich, he looked bored, as if he were sick to death of making fortunes on the stock exchange. He thought it came off rather well.

From the periphery of his vision, Apple saw the girl removing her gloves. He felt dull again. That act, he thought, might well mean that Sylvia had come to the end of her session of work.

But he went on. His gaze he kept high. Nearing Sylvia, he pretended to see the warning sign for the first time. He performed the facial shrug of a man who doesn't care about money and gave the pertinent part of his clothing one light tap with a forefinger.

By the time Apple was within two strides of the mystery girl, his hand was back behind him and he was looking with interest at the low ceiling's water stains.

Apple sensed rather than saw Sylvia cross his path. At the same moment, her basket brushed heavily against his left arm and he felt a soft movement rippling over the right side of his chest.

Next, the girl had gone. Still moving, Apple hoped he

wasn't mistaken, and, pressing inward with his right bicep, felt the emptiness that told him he wasn't. He had been successful in accomplishing a loss of wallet.

Relaxed, smiling with the inside of his mouth, Apple went on at a stroll. He lit a cigarette grandly and assured himself that he was a cool one all right. He had played that bit of business just so.

Self-congratulation over, Apple wondered what he ought to do now. His mentor, the flashy Ned, was nowhere to be seen. And it would probably be a mistake to try to check on what had become of Sylvia. After all, he was supposed to be a pickpocket's victim. If he stayed around, he would need to put on a show of outrage.

Apple stopped walking. Slowly, the fact was penetrating that he had, in fact, been a victim of a pickpocket. He had lost a wallet which held papers, credit cards, cash and a blank check, plus a photograph of Monico standing beside Ethel. He had been robbed.

Apple tossed away his cigarette and headed firmly for the stairs.

As Apple went into the reception room of the front called Trident Imports, its inner door opened. Through the frame came, first, a mumble of voices which Apple recognised as being via radio; next, after a pause, Angus Watkin.

Apple's Control, looking drab in a lounge suit, greeted the visitor with a bland nod before closing the door behind him. Which reminded Apple that he had left his own door open. He closed it.

"Thank you, Porter," Angus Watkin said. "Are we a trifle absent-minded due to nervousness?"

"No, sir. Not at all."

"Not at all which, absent-minded or nervous?"

"Neither, sir," Apple said, hating healthily. "It's simply that I wasn't sure whether I was supposed to come back here or not."

"You were, Porter. If, that is, you have had your pocket picked."

"I have, sir."

"By the right person?"

"I have been led to believe so."

"Good," Angus Watkin said. "Please be seated." He waved generously at a chair, which Apple took. "And, just on the off chance that you were concerned about your purloined property, which I don't suppose for a minute you were, let me assure you that it is quite safe."

"Thank you, sir."

"I hope."

"Ah," Apple said.

"But I do believe I hear our client's hackney carriage now, below in Baker Street."

After a mental blink of surprise, Apple dismissed his idea that the conviction he had always held regarding Watkin—that he was totally void of humour—had been proven wrong. This was simply another of his chief's methods of keeping an underling on the alert with the unexpected.

Listening to the same footfalls in the hall that had triggered Angus Watkin's shot at wit, Apple decided against firing back the fact that, despite popular belief, nowhere in his canon did Sir Arthur Conan Doyle have Sherlock Holmes say "Elementary, my dear Watson." It might not help.

The outer door opened. In came Ned, who had one hand hidden inside his gaudy jacket in the style of Napoleon. He said, "All okay, sir."

"Good," Watkin said. "Let's have it."

Ned brought his hand out. The finger and thumb delicately held a wallet, which, Apple could see, was his own. Ned passed it over to Angus Watkin, who took it with equal care and said, "You will have your property returned to you presently, Porter." He turned to the inner door, leaving on a dull "Good day, Ned."

"Good day, sir," the flashily dressed man said. After giving Apple a wink and tipping him a forefinger salute, he left the office.

Apple knew that most likely he and Ned would never meet again—at least, professionally. There was an outside chance that, even among London's millions, they would see one another, on the street or in a cinema or wherever the human animal ranges. If so, each would look right through the other. There was a more remote chance, though not too long a shot, that someday they would find themselves at the same social gathering. If so, they would chat without a hint to one another that they had ever met before.

The dwelling on which with his mind's surface had given Apple the time to work out on a lower strata the business with the mystery girl.

It was typical of Watkin, he thought, that he would kill two sea-gulls with one rock. Sylvia was tested for dipping skill on a tall man at the same time her fingerprints were being obtained—on the wallet that Ned had wiped clean on his sleeve before returning to Apple's pocket, the wallet that had been stolen by Sylvia, and then stolen back from Sylvia by genius Ned.

All of which went to prove the value of need-to-know, Apple acknowledged. If he had been privy to what was going to happen, he might have acted quite differently, and therefore negatively.

In another minute Angus Watkin returned to the of-

fice. He gave Apple his wallet back and said, "Thank you,
Porter. That will be all. Good day."

Still sitting, because he knew that his Control, like
most men, didn't like to be towered over, Apple said, "I
hope you don't mind my asking . . ."

"Why all the elaborations to procure latent prints? I
do, but we'll let that pass. I'm all in favour of nosiness.
You've never had enough of it, Porter."

"No, sir."

Angus Watkin said, "The point is, the lady always
wears her gloves except when actually doing her
pickpocketing work. Another arousal of my suspicion,
that, although it could of course be passed off as the desire
or need to protect those clever hands."

"Like a violinist."

"Precisely. She even wears gloves when at home, in
her Earl's Court flat. At any rate, we found no prints there
when we turned the place over."

"That's being a bit too careful, isn't it, sir?"

"Perhaps," Angus Watkin said. "However, Sylvia's
passport tells us that she arrived some days ago from Melbourne, and Australia House has told us that the passport
is genuine. But both mean very little."

"Landlord?" Apple suggested. "Other tenants?"

Watkin shook his head. "We daren't risk giving our-
selves away by snooping, Porter."

"Of course not. Silly of me. We have to tread softly if
the lady is a Sickle."

"True, Porter, and perhaps you can tell me why."

Apple fumbled, "Well, sir, if she is KGB—um—"

Angus Watkin finished, "And if she knows we're on to
her game, she will close it down and dissolve, in my opinion, just to keep us away. Which means what, Porter?"

"I don't know, sir."

"That the winner's prize would be more damaging to the opposition in our hands than it would be beneficial to them in theirs."

"I see, sir," Apple said. He risked, "But what is the game and what is the prize?"

Almost betraying pleasure, Angus Watkin said, "I haven't the slightest idea. The prize is possibly information. The game is possibly looking for it, for a letter-drop used by the late Narkov, or the place where he hid it when he thought that we were on to him."

"And possibly, sir, the lady is straight."

"That's doubtful. Too many jars. Not least among which is the perfection of her cover role. That's very KGB. If she had appeared on the scene in the guise of a reporter, or a new railway employee, or any of half-a-dozen other parts, Moscow would expect us to be suspicious."

Apple said, "But being outside the law, a pickpocket, the Reds would think that'd put the blinkers on us."

"Just so."

"It also explains, and very satisfactorily, her lingering presence."

"True. Altogether too neat, in fact. Even so, as has been said, the lady might be genuine. Perhaps we'll have a better idea when Interpol and Australia and various others get back to us on her fingerprints."

"What if, meanwhile, she wins the prize, sir?"

"She's being watched by some of my people," Angus Watkin said, brusque now. "They are in touch here by walkie-talkie." He clasped his hands together like a vicar. "And that, Porter, is all. Good day."

Apple rose into a tall crouch. He risked on, "But why, sir, doesn't an operative make an approach, try to establish contact?"

"Would be useful if one could, Porter, I agree. Yet that would be almost impossible without rousing suspicion. You don't suppose, do you, that Sylvia would be interested in letting some man pick her up?"

"Well no, sir, of course not."

"Good *day*, Porter."

Like someone who had been refused admission to the cheapest brothel in town, Apple clumped glumly down the stairs. He was empty, despondent. The job and the involvement and the shop talk, brief though they had been, had filled him with a mild euphoria. This, he knew, came from a combination of sources: a sense of belonging, a feeling of purpose and the pleasure of conspiracy.

Now Apple felt like a player in team sports who gets sent off right at the beginning of that important match. Furthermore he felt like a lover who is granted only one short look at his mistress.

Changing to a swift, jogging descent, Apple denied to himself that he was smitten with the mystery girl. Such an idea was absurd, stupid, insane. He couldn't possibly be, not on so brief and distant an acquaintance, without either a word or a glance exchanged. Professionally intrigued, certainly. Smitten, no.

Apple, going out onto Regent Street, firmly gave his mind to the matter of his next move, now that the job was finished. Should he grab a sandwich or have a full lunch before going back to the Manx composition?

Apple was indifferent to the question of eating, but reacted to its follow-up. At this moment the United Kingdom Philological Institute stifled him even in thought.

Sighing, Apple mused that it might have been better if he had never been given that job to do.

Apple came alert with a snap. He saw that he had

stopped walking, found that he was at the top of the steps descending to Piccadilly Station, realised that he wanted to go down.

Why not? he thought. It wouldn't hurt. He could have a short stroll around, one circuit, revive the belonging and purpose and conspiracy. But he might feel even worse afterwards. Also, it wasn't professionally kosher. Also number two, he would be sure to be seen by the girl.

Which, of course, wouldn't matter if he changed his appearance sufficiently.

Apple swung around.

Seven minutes later, stimulated, he was back at the head of the steps. He was wearing the sun-glasses he had just bought. His tie was off and, in the style favoured by provincials on holiday, he had his open shirt collar lying out over the collar of his suit jacket. He felt pleasantly daring.

Descending in a sag at the knees, shoulders rounded, Apple joined the station's milling crowd. He was only half a head taller than the average, but half blind because of the dark glasses. Face down, he peered over their tops.

When he caught sight of Sylvia, Apple moved to the wall. He leaned there, which rendered his body's slump less unnatural. Between looks at the mystery girl, he glanced about to try to pinpoint Watkin's people. He was able to pick out two or three possible operatives.

Sylvia acted as though she were waiting for someone, but without impatience. At regular intervals she checked her watch and made brief, slow wanders away from and back to her standing place. These short strolls, Apple surmised, would be to pick somebody's pocket, although he saw nothing suspect in her actions.

A voice close at hand asked evenly, "What d'you think you're playing at?"

Apple turned his head. Beside him was a man of about his own age and of close to his present reduced height. He had curly hair and the features of a boxer who knew more about taking than giving. Broad shoulders stretched tight a black leather wind-cheater.

With relief, Apple dismissed the notion that this was an Upstairs agent. Over his sun-glasses he peered amiably at the tough-looking man, who said, "That disguise wouldn't fool a backward mole, mate. I seen you here a while back. Couldn't miss a long drink of water like you, could I?"

If doubtful of what to say, say nothing. Thus ran the adage which, with many others, had been drummed into Apple during his training days. So he smiled.

"Cocky, eh?" the man said. He gave his shoulders several quick shrugs. "Well, let me tell you something, tall-arse. This here 'Dilly pitch is chock-a-block. There's no room for outsiders. If you try dipping around here you might find yourself with a broken arm."

With some surprise, and a great deal of delight, Apple realised that this heavy character had taken him for a pickpocket. He gazed all around in an unconscious search for witnesses—and was just in time to see Sylvia going from view.

The man asked, "Get me, flag-pole?"

Speaking in Italian, Apple told the man while straightening from his lean that he didn't understand English but it had been a pleasure, a real pleasure, and they must do it again sometime. He bowed and moved on.

Coming within view of Sylvia, Apple saw that she had donned her gloves and was turning onto one of the flights of steps, ascending. He followed, staying well back. He didn't bother to ask himself what he thought he was doing.

Up on the street, in the noon brightness, Apple had no need to peer over his sun-glasses. He walked erect as he trailed the mystery girl along Shaftesbury Avenue. He noted cheerfully that she had an excellent figure and decent calves.

After a moment it occurred to Apple that here was a golden opportunity. Angus Watkin had said that it would be useful if an agent could establish a personal contact with Sylvia. So why didn't underling Appleton Porter try to do just that?—and get in on this operation while at the same time shooting up in his chief's estimation.

Because, Apple answered, Watkin had also said that it would be impossible without rousing the girl's suspicion, which would probably blow the whole caper.

Even so, Apple thought about it.

He was still thinking, and still getting nowhere, when Sylvia, having turned into Soho, entered a cafeteria. Apple started to cross to the other side of the street, where he intended taking up a watch.

He held as a pedal bike went by; then did a double take at its rider. The teenager was wearing a black leather wind-cheater like that stretched by the heavy in Piccadilly Station.

Got it, Apple thought, elated and grinning.

Turning, he went to one of the cafeteria's windows. He covered the final few feet with caution. From an angle he looked inside. Sylvia was sliding a tray along the rails beside the self-service counter.

Watching, Apple congratulated himself on his idea. It was brilliant. Sylvia couldn't possibly suspect an enemy— if, that is, she was an enemy herself, which was in doubt.

Paying, the girl took her tray to a vacant table. Her crockery—cup and saucer, plate holding a sandwich—she set out and then put the tray in a rack.

Apple went on watching after Sylvia had sat down. He wanted to see if there were any signals to be read by a fellow agent: approach, stay clear, I am under observation. These and a host of others could be transmitted by various positions of the person's body, crockery, chairs, cutlery, objects such as ashtrays.

Everything seeming to be straightforward, Apple moved towards the entrance. As he went, he took off and put away his dark glasses, righted his shirt collar, brought out his tie. He was still straightening the knot when, inside the cafeteria, he stopped by Sylvia's table.

She looked up at him blankly. Smiling, he asked, "Do you remember me?"

"No," Sylvia said. "I certainly do not." She had a faint accent that could have been Australian, New Zealand or South African.

Apple said, "Doesn't matter. May I sit down? Thank you." He sat without waiting for a word or sign of invitation, pleased by his lack of graciousness. "Who I am doesn't matter. It's *what* that counts."

"Please leave this table."

"And what I am," Apple said, "is a dip."

The mystery girl gazed at him steadily. There was nothing to be read in her blue eyes. She might have been trying to choose from a menu which had on offer only dishes that she found boring.

It was the kind of cool, Apple thought, that training in espionage created. He said, "If you don't remember me, you may remember this." He brought out his wallet. "You dipped it off me about half an hour ago, down in the 'Dilly station."

That produced a response. The girl's nostrils

twitched, her eyes flicked down toward the shopping basket standing beside her chair.

"Yes," Apple said, "I got it from there." He winked. "I dipped you back, a few minutes later. But I only took my own property. Nothing else. Check and see."

"I don't know what you're talking about," the girl said, but she had been having a good, close look at the wallet Apple was holding.

Putting it away casually, he began to talk. The tone he kept friendly. She needn't bother to go on bluffing, he said, for there was nothing to worry about. He wasn't a cop. As he had already told her, he was a pickpocket. And there was nothing more embarrassing for a dip than to be dipped himself. Also annoying.

"But I recovered from that," Apple went on, "once I'd got my wallet back. I realised what a pro you were. It takes real talent to lift something from a man my height. So I went back to look for you, and followed you here."

Sylvia, still blank of face, asked, "Why did you look for me and follow me?"

Apple spread his hands. "Well, just to say congratulations. And now I'll say it. Congratulations. You are a star performer, Sylvia."

On realising his mistake, Apple dropped his hands out of sight and, as though he were looking at the basket, he turned his face downward.

The girl asked, "Why did you call me that?"

Apple looked up smiling, recovering. He said, "Simply because it fits."

"Really?"

"Yes. That's the type you are. You look as free and lovely as the wild woods. The name relates to 'forest-dweller,' you see."

"Well now."

"It also might interest you to know that its masculine form is Sylvanus."

At last the girl's face relaxed enough to show emotion. She looked flattered and intrigued, though both in restrained degree. She said, "Thanks for the compliment. The second one. The first isn't valid, as you'll find out if you take a look inside my basket." She gave a faint smile. "It's empty."

Apple felt a twinge of doubt. "Empty?"

"So perhaps you've got the wrong person."

"Oh. But I can't have."

Abruptly, Sylvia produced a full, rich smile. Her whole face joined in the act. Eyes twinkling as brightly as the glints from her white, shiny teeth, she said, "All right, bluff over. But I bet I could've got away with it if I'd wanted."

"Yes, I believe you could," Apple said, relieved. "Is your basket really empty?"

"Sure. I never leave a dipping scene in possession of the evidence. I've got what counts—the bread." She patted between her ample breasts. "The wallets, I got shot of them in the station."

"Where abouts?"

Sylvia's smile congealed slightly. "In the usual place, of course," she said. "A lavatory flush-box in the loo. You don't *keep* yours, do you?"

He had made another mistake, Apple knew, and this time he would have to use the second of the two standard methods of recovery. The first was with flattery, the second with something like the reverse.

"Well," he said, acting pale diffidence, "I don't mind taking a mark's bread, but I think it's wrong to deprive him of all his papers and so forth. Some documents can be irreplaceable."

Sylvia blinked slowly. "I see."

"So what I do is, I drop the wallets in a post-box. They finish up in Lost Property."

"That's good of you."

"Oh, I don't know."

"And bad of me," the girl said. "But it's always safety first as far as I'm concerned."

Apple nodded, glad that his recovery had worked. "You're more sensible than I am. My routine could trip me up one of these days."

He leaned back. Sylvia did the same. They regarded one another in a comfortable silence. The mystery girl's face seemed to reflect what Apple was feeling: a cautious satisfaction.

"So," Sylvia said, "we happen to be in the same line of business."

Apple said, "Yes, but I'm interrupting your lunch."

"That's all right. And you could always join me, get yourself something."

"I'll do that . . . What do I call you?"

"Why not Sylvia? I like it. It's certainly a lot nicer than Betty."

"That's your real name?"

"It claims so on my passport," Sylvia said. "The meat pies here are very good."

"Don't go away," Apple said, rising. He went towards the counter. That he felt a fraction taller than normal didn't bother him in the least. It didn't show. He was high on the inside, with success.

While waiting in line with a tray, Apple stopped himself from looking around for signs of Watkin's people. There was, he felt, sure to be at least one observer. That was fine so long as he could maintain the relationship with

Sylvia. If he didn't, this interference of his could well mean that he would never work for Intelligence again.

Apple left that thought. He reminded himself of how clever he had been to call the girl by her code-name so that he could follow it with a bit of flattery.

With a meat pie (flattery of a more subtle nature) plus a mug of chicken soup, Apple went back to the table. As soon as he was settled, Sylvia startled him by asking, "So what do I call you?"

He hadn't given a thought to cover. Filling his mouth with pie as a delayer, he quickly flitted his mind around, found nothing ready-made and conveniently waiting, and decided to stick close to the truth. It would include, if necessary, the United Kingdom Philological Institute. He could always say he needed to pick pockets because of the paltry wage he earned there.

"Russ," Apple said after swallowing. For his own sake he added, "It's short for Russell."

"That's a nice name," Sylvia said. She put the last piece of sandwich in her mouth and brushed crumbs off her gloved hands.

Apple asked, partly to get the subject away from himself, "Are you that much afraid of damage to the tools of your trade?"

Chewing, Sylvia shook her head. She swallowed and said, "Not the least bit. Damage doesn't bother me too much. I wear gloves all the time to keep my hands sensitive. Which they are to an amazing degree. With one knuckle I can tell serge from tweed."

"You're a natural, Sylvia."

"Maybe inherited. I was born to dip."

"And where did that happen?" Apple asked, looking into his soup as if that were more interesting than his question. "You sound a bit Aussiefied."

"On the nose. Melbourne."

Between sips of tea, Sylvia went on to tell of working with her pickpocket father when she was a child and as she grew up. They worked all the larger Australian towns. After his death two years ago, when she was twenty, she had gone abroad and kept on the move.

"I got here a few days ago, Russ. And business has been fair. But on the topic of business."

The trade talk that followed, Apple followed only with difficulty. He faked it, hoping to stay lucky. It seemed that he did, for there were no blank responses to his grunts and mumbles, head-shakes and smiled affirmatives.

At last, while he was supplying a light for their cigarettes, Apple got clear with, "Are you going back to work from here?"

"No. Home to nap. It was a busy morning."

"Well, look, Sylvia, why don't we get together again this evening?"

She smiled. "To work together, you mean? Yes, I think that's a neat idea."

That had not been what he had meant, but it was a move in the right direction, so there was nothing for it except for him to give another of those mumbles.

"Maybe we can learn from each other, Russ. You're clever. I never even saw you when you took your wallet back."

"They used to call me the lofty ghost."

"You're tall all right," Sylvia said. "My father was too, well over six feet. But it made him memorable, so he had to keep moving. And talking of moving."

While on their way out to the street, they agreed to meet at six o'clock, here, where it was convenient for Piccadilly Circus. Sylvia offered a gloved hand to be shaken. She was friendly but reserved.

Watching her walk away, Apple accepted that yes, he was smitten. He didn't know if it had been due to the smile, the blue eyes, the figure or what, but smitten he was. And that, he realised, could be awkward. If Sylvia wasn't an enemy agent, she was a common thief. He didn't know which he preferred.

Turning, Apple walked on, heading deeper into the narrow streets of Soho. The first thing he had to do now, he mused, was call in, contact Angus Watkin and explain what had happened, though undoubtedly Watkin would already know most of it.

Apple thought there was a good chance of his Control being still at the phony office on Regent Street. However, for one thing, to go there uninvited was bad form; for a more important thing, a telephone conversation was preferable to a face-to-face meeting with Watkin after this interference in the caper he was running.

Apple was wondering how Angus Watkin, the king of the bland, would manifest anger, when he heard the squeal of car brakes coupled with a scream of warning.

TWO

Up the kerb came the car. It came towards Apple. He saw this from over his right shoulder as he reacted to the shrill noise. Next, one-third of a second later, he reacted to the sight. He hurled himself in the other direction.

There was a stretch of wall between shops. Apple hit it with his hands, which he then used to push his body into a frantic, swirling turn.

Shoulders now to the wall, Apple froze—all except for his heart, which went on pounding. The car had stopped.

Aware dimly of a rising jabber of voices and the approach of people, Apple gaped his relief at the large blue Daimler. It stood half on the roadway, half on the pavement. Inside the opulent limousine, in front, were a man and a woman. The woman was the driver.

She started to reverse the car slowly as people pushed in front of Apple and blocked his view. That made him realise he had semi-sunk to a fighting stance. He stayed there, listening to his heart slow back to normal, licking the dryness away from his lips, assuring enquirers that he was unhurt.

The people, looking either disappointed or offended, were beginning to disperse, and Apple had straightened to a high sag on the wall when the couple from the Daimler came up at a bustle.

About fifty years old, well-dressed, they were lean

and tanned like nudists who daily jogged their way to the health-food store. They also looked rich enough to have fat servants.

The woman, flapping her hands as if she wanted a towel, appeared to be distraught. The man had an expression of contained annoyance. He said briskly to Apple, "You're perfectly all right, I see. That's good. Fine. Marvellous. No harm done. Nothing to fuss about."

Before he had finished, the woman was asking, "Are you hurt, you poor thing? Are you terribly shattered? Is there anything broken, young man?"

"He's fine, darling," the man said.

"No, darling, he's quite white."

"He just said he was perfectly all right."

"I didn't say a word," Apple said. "But I am okay, as a matter of fact." This, now, was true.

The man took a step backwards. "You see, darling. He just happens to be the white type."

"Really, darling."

"Now do let's get on."

Flapping a hand at him, the woman asked Apple anxiously, "You're not going to report this to the police, are you?"

"Of course not."

"It wasn't my fault really. In a way. There was a dear little kitten crossing the road. What would you have done?" Without waiting for an answer, she began to insist on driving Apple home and asked him for his address, the man meanwhile looking repeatedly at the sky and muttering, "He's quite all right, darling."

Apple gave his address to end the repetition. He said, "But I'm not going there from here. And I don't need to be driven anyway."

"Oh, but you do, young man, and you must go. You

must lie in a darkened room with a damp cloth on your brow."

"I can assure you, ma'am," Apple said, firm, "that I am totally unhurt."

The man tugged at his companion's sleeve. "Do let's get along, darling."

But she talked on: apologising, describing the kitten, saying how silly and officious the police could be, promising to send black grapes.

Apple grew bored. Politeness, however, kept him standing there. He tuned out the fussy voice and let his mind go to where it wanted to be, on Sylvia, being as objective as he could under the smitten circumstances.

That passport crack of hers, Apple mused, which hinted at theft or forgery, seemed too open for her to be KGB. But she was as cool as a Sickle would be on a mission. Her reason for wearing gloves all the time did have the ring of truth. But would a thief speak in so educated a manner? On the other hand, her way of talking about her father had a pleasant, understated naturalness.

Apple, brought back from his muse by an insistent tone, asked, "I beg your pardon?"

The woman said, "Perhaps we should take you to a pub and get you a brandy."

Apple shook his head, the man sighed heavily at the sky, and his flustered companion switched back to the offer of a drive home.

This time, what stopped Apple from tuning out was seeing the man's actions. He was patting his pockets in impatience. Apple remembered a factor which had slipped his main attention earlier, in the excitement of having established contact with the mystery girl.

Tonight he was expected to be a pickpocket.

After digesting that with unhappy nods, Apple realised what most likely lay behind Sylvia's suggestion. It would be a test for the tall man who called himself Russ and claimed to be a dip. Thief or Sickle, Sylvia wanted to find out if he was genuine. So: he had to shine this evening as a star picker of pockets.

The woman asked, "Are you feeling all right, young man?"

Edging off sideways, Apple fumbled that he was late, he had to go to work, he was feeling fine, he would look forward to the black grapes, he—

Turned and ran.

Less than one minute later Apple was in a public telephone-box on a street corner. The door held slightly open with a foot because of his claustrophobia, he dialled a series of numbers. A cool male voice answered. Apple gave two more sets of numbers to identify both himself and the person he wished to speak to.

After a pause, the voice of Angus Watkin asked, "What took you so long to call in?"

"Well—"

"You left the cafeteria eight minutes ago, Porter. But possibly you had to wait your turn to use the telephone. Never mind now. Get on with it. Report."

"Yes, sir."

"We will leave until another time the question of disciplinary action."

So Apple began at the end instead of the beginning: "I am meeting Sylvia at six o'clock this evening, sir. We have a date." Not waiting for a comment from his Control, he went straight ahead with a recounting of all that had taken place in the cafeteria. He ended near the beginning, with, "Before that, I happened to see her up on the street, and followed. Talking to her was one of those spur-

of-the-moment things. You might even call it inspiration
—that idea for an approach that came to me."

Angus Watkin asked in his dull brown voice, "Like a
bolt out of the blue, mayhap?"

Apple chose to treat the question as straight, not as
the buckled blade of sarcasm. "I think one could certainly
say that, sir, yes."

"Which bolt, fortunately, you were able to see despite
your dark glasses?"

This question Apple chose to ignore, apart from telling himself in passing that he might have known. He said,
"But we have two problems. One is my cover."

"There's nothing wrong with the cover you have already, Porter. If politicians can try their hands at bur-
glary, and doctors pull off the occasional murder, a philol-
ogist can surely be a pickpocket."

"I thought of that, sir, yes, but there's the name. I told
Sylvia my first name was Russell, not Appleton. Russ for
short. She might check."

"Why that name particularly?"

Knowing that his chief knew, and hating him for
making him go through with this, Apple explained, "Some
people, it seems, call me Russet."

Watkin drawled, "Why is that?"

Apple winced with every word of, "It's because I
sometimes, occasionally, under certain circumstances, at
particular moments, tend to blush. Faintly."

"An espionage agent who blushes?" Angus Watkin
murmured. "That's hard to believe."

Through gritted teeth Apple said, "Very good, sir, I'll
stick with my own cover and get around the name thing."

"Do, Porter."

"The next problem is the pickpocketing I'm supposed to do tonight with Sylvia. What I need is an excuse to get me out of having to go through with it."

"An excuse would be far too suspicious," Angus Watkin said. "That is definitely out. You will have to pick pockets."

"I can't, sir."

"You took a course in that art, did you not, at Damian House?"

"Only the basics, sir. Crude stuff. And I've told Sylvia I'm a top-flight pro. When she sees I'm not, that'll be the end. Obviously, she's testing me."

From the other end of the line, silence. Apple asked, "Are you there, sir?"

"Yes," Angus Watkin said. "Return to base. At once. Stay there. I'll be in touch. Goodbye, Porter."

From Soho to Bloomsbury is a mere stretch of the legs. Apple stretched his in long, fast strides. He didn't know if the urgency he sensed was of his own making, or if he had read it, mistakenly or otherwise, in Watkin's crisp orders. Whichever, he felt better to be moving at a good clip.

Probably, his feeling was composed of relief and excitement, Apple mused. He could have been fired, or pulled out fast enough to give him whiplash. Instead, he was solidly in. In on a caper. All he had to do now was make sure he didn't blow it. This one could be a cracker.

Smiling distantly, Apple allowed himself to drift into a reverie.

He is sitting on a couch, an arm around Sylvia. Lighting is supplied by candles. Music plays softly, seductively. Apple whispers, "May I tell you something, Syl?" Her blue eyes warm with devotion, Sylvia nods. Apple says, "Russell is actually my middle name."

Back in the present, more or less, Apple decided that the mystery girl could easily turn out to be neither an enemy agent nor a professional thief. She was merely playing at being a pickpocket, for some odd reason.

When no reason occurred to him immediately, Apple left the matter there with blithe unconcern. He changed from striding to jogging.

Two blocks past the British Museum, Apple came to the handsome Edwardian building called Harlequin Mansions. He went into the entrance hallway and up three flights of carpeted stairs. As always, there was nothing to be heard from the various apartments.

Apple turned onto his own corridor. There, for the second time within thirty minutes, he froze.

Ten yards along, a man was reversing out of a doorway. That was normal; people often left their flats that way to make sure the door was securely locked. But in this case the flat belonged to Apple.

Through his head raced all the possible explanations of legitimacy, from landlord to neighbour, from telephone repairman to window-washer. Nothing fitted. He was left with only one solution: burglar.

More piqued than disturbed, Apple began to move forward. This, he thought, would never have happened if it hadn't been for stupid rules against domestic pets. The would-be intruder would have been frightened off by Monico's heavy gasping.

After pulling the door closed, the man turned. He did what Apple had done a few seconds ago—snapped to a halt. His expression clicked to nothingness.

He was in his early thirties, soberly but untidily dressed. Close-cropped hair complemented a face of severe features, like a rock on a brick. Though narrow across the shoulders, he was deep in the chest.

Apple kept moving forward. He strode tall and firm. His annoyance had grown due to the seeming lack of fear in the intruder, who now seeped to life.

He walked this way. His body manner was casual, his gaze was directed to somewhere beyond Apple, as if they were on a street. He wore an expression of mild boredom.

When they were separated by three or four strides, Apple snapped, "Not so fast." That, he told himself, was the regulation thing to say in these cases.

The man ignored him. He came level and began to go past. Apple grabbed his arm.

The fight was on.

Which came as a surprise to Apple. He had always had the vague idea that burglars made statements like, "All right, guv, it's a fair cop, I'll come along quiet." He was totally unprepared for the punch.

It caught him on the left temple. He staggered aside, but with a wild grab managed to catch the man by the lapel. Using that, he was able to pull himself back into balance—and be in position to receive the next punch.

It landed in his belly. Breath oofed out of him as he doubled over. But he retained his grip.

The man was trying to pull away. At the same time, he was flinging upper-cuts. Apple saw them as they came into his down-aimed vision and was able to dodge.

There was silence in the hall apart from the sounds of scuffling and panting. Apple had the weird sensation of being an intruder himself. He would have shouted, in hopes of being heard by a neighbour, who would then call the police, except for feeling that this would be a weakness on his part.

Breath recovered, Apple pushed up and back. During the act he accidentally thumped his opponent under the chin with the top of his head.

It didn't even stall the man. He began throwing one-two combinations. Due to his being held off, they all landed on Apple's upper chest.

Swinging his arm up, Apple brought a judo chop down onto the side of the intruder's neck. The perfection of the blow gave him a thrill. Confident, he released his hold on the lapel.

The man drew back a round-house right. Apple covered with both forearms. But, instead of a punch on high, he got a kick in the ankle. He yelped at the agony.

The intruder ran.

Apple gave feeble chase. Holding his wounded leg doubled up, he hopped along the corridor. He was still yelping between shouts at the man to stop in the name of the law.

Unheedful, the man whipped around onto the staircase and was gone. Stairs Apple couldn't manage in his pain. He hopped on to the end of the corridor, whimpering now, and then began to hop his way back.

A door opened. An older woman looked out. She said, "Oh, it's you."

"Yes," Apple gasped, hopping by with a polite smile. "Good afternoon, Mrs. Entwhistle."

"Good afternoon, Mr. Porter." The door closed.

His reputation as an eccentric was at last firmly made, Apple thought, cheering up. So all was well that ended well, as long as the burglar hadn't caused too much damage—which thieves were said to do if they could find nothing of value, and the man had been empty-handed.

Naturally enough, Apple mused while putting his leg down gently. There was no object in the flat of any value save the sentimental.

Pain easing, Apple limped to his door. He let himself in, went along the passage and started to look around.

On finding no damage, Apple's cheer flourished. However, as he made a second tour of the various large, high-ceilinged rooms, he became pensive.

There was absolutely nothing out of place.

The strangeness of that gave Apple an eerie feeling, quite apart from that faint discomfort brought by the spoor. His cheer fled.

To be sure, Apple went around his flat a third time. He kept his hands afted so that he wouldn't unthinkingly touch anything. Finally, his worst suspicions were confirmed by seeing that the wardrobe door was slightly ajar; he recalled having left it like that on Friday, in his hurry to get away.

As Apple headed for the telephone, on a corner table in his living-room, he reflected how fortunate it was that Monico had not, after all, been at home. An espionage operative would have killed him without a moment's hesitation.

When Apple opened his flat door he found outside, unexpectedly, two people. The man and woman, standing one behind the other, were both strangers.

The man, foremost, had a finger held to his lips.

He was young, tall, and of the type called clean-cut. In his blazer and flannels he might have been on his way to the vicarage to play croquet.

Taking his hand away from his mouth, he gestured: go back inside. That Apple obeyed, turning, was because Angus Watkin had said on the telephone fifteen minutes ago, "I'll send someone along who'll know what to do."

Where doorways began to open off the main passage, the man pointed to the living room before going into the kitchen. Again Apple obeyed. He was followed by the woman, who glanced about with acute interest, like an early bird.

She was middle-aged and dumpy, wearing sensible shoes and a tweed suit. Her spectacles had been repaired on one arm with sticking plaster. She could have played perfectly the part of the vicar's wife, wondering where she had put the balls.

Despite being depressed, Apple remembered his hostmanship. He silently got the woman's attention and made offering motions towards a chair. After shrugging indifferently, she sat.

Apple was depressed because if, as he was 90 per cent sure was the case, the intruder was a spy, that meant he had been rumbled by the opposition. Angus Watkin would have to pull him out.

The clean-cut type came into the living-room. He spent less than two minutes poking about like a sanitary inspector. Straightening from a peer under the carpet, he said, as though with resignation, "Clean."

So, Apple thought, the intruder hadn't been here to plant bugs. "Thanks."

" 'Bye," the man said. He left.

The woman got up. "I'll start here, if it's all the same to you."

Apple bowed. "Help yourself." He didn't know what she was talking about. But then, he hadn't known what the man was up to until he had pronounced cleanliness.

Apple left the room and went to his kitchen. There, he came across more of the unexpected. Sitting at the centre table was Angus Watkin.

He said, "That young man let me in."

"That's fine, sir," Apple said. "Er—the woman." It was a question.

"She, Porter, is looking for what the police refer to as

a calling-card. By which they mean a burglar's personal method of entry and search. He gives himself away by sticking to the tried and true."

"My man wouldn't have had any trouble with locks."

"No, and in our case we only want to know which organisation gave the orders, not the identity of its agent. Often the manner of searching can tell us that. If the calling-card is here, the lady will undoubtedly find it. Women have a flair for these things."

Apple nodded glumly. But, again remembering his position as host, he asked, "Would you like some tea, sir?"

"No, thank you," Angus Watkin said following a dubious look around the kitchen. "Sit down, please. Tell me about the couple with the car."

Apple sat opposite his chief. "They were very clever," he said, in truth, not merely to excuse himself for having fallen for the gimmick.

"Really, Porter?"

"Yes, sir. They performed jester and knave perfectly. A real Mutt and Jeff. The woman clung, the man tried to get away. They even played it anti-police. I gave my address without stopping to consider."

"Yes, the old trick still works," Angus Watkin said. "At least, under certain circumstances." The implication seemed to be that the circumstances were created by the victim's gullibility. "Describe the couple, please."

While Apple was doing this, the vicar's wife came in, stopping on the threshold. She said, "Excuse me."

Watkin waved a gracious hand. "Proceed."

"The signs are quite clear, sir."

"Good."

"It was a CIA job."

"You're sure?"

"I'd swear to it."

"Thank you," Angus Watkin said with a long nod. "Good afternoon."

"Afternoon, sir," the woman said. She left.

Apple, his spirits on the climb, began, "If it was the Mayflowers . . ."

"And it was, if the lady says so. Which means one, that I have to start going through channels to see if I can call off the Central Intelligence Agency, and two, that I don't have to pull you out."

Apple sighed. "Yes, sir."

"They saw you with Sylvia, of course," Watkin said, "and decided to try finding out what your game is, because, like us, they want to know what *her* game is."

"Exactly, sir. Are you quite sure you wouldn't like a cup of tea?"

"I am absolutely positive, Porter. Let us stick to the matter in hand."

"Sorry, sir," Apple said, looking suitably contrite about the eyes to curry whatever favour he could.

His Control said, "The returns from Sylvia's fingerprints, you should know, are inconclusive. In other words, she isn't known to the police authorities anywhere."

Keenly, eyes a shade narrowed, Apple pointed out, "That, however, doesn't necessarily signify that she isn't a genuine criminal."

"True, Porter. We are, in fact, at about the same stage as we were this morning."

"Except, sir, that a personal contact has now been forged with Sylvia."

Ignoring that, Angus Watkin said, "Nor are the young lady's prints on any of our own files. Which, again, does not mean that she isn't KGB. Therefore, Porter, it looks as if it's up to you to play detective."

"I shall do my very best, sir."

After a short silence, Watkin said, "In respect of your test this evening, I am going to arrange for an imitation victim. I shall use Ned, whom you have already met. You see what I mean, Porter?"

"Yes, sir. A brilliant idea, if I may say so. Ned will let me pick his pocket."

"Quite. After that, you will get out of further work by claiming to see a policeman who knows you, or being bored by the lack of challenge, or whatever occurs to you."

"I'll think of something, sir," Apple said. "The most important thing is for Ned to be in the Piccadilly Station when we arrive."

Angus Watkin closed his eyes briefly before saying, "I doubt very much if you and the young lady will be going to that particular place."

"But that was my understanding."

"No doubt, Porter. If, however, this is a test of your bona fides, and it probably is, whether the lady be white or Red, she will anticipate the possibility of an arranged victim, don't you think?"

"I do now, sir," Apple said, currying heartily. "I didn't before."

"Therefore the young lady will say something along the lines of 'Let's go to Otherplace, it gets so windy in the Piccadilly underground at night.' "

"Then Ned, in fact, will follow us."

Watkin nodded. "That's something you need to know because you must take care not to lose him in the traffic."

Apple asked, "Traffic, sir?" It wasn't solely to make his chief happy with a question.

"If the suggested place of operations is not at hand," Angus Watkin said, "you will drive."

"I see. I'm to be given a car."

"No, you are not, Porter. You will use your own means of transportation."

"Ethel?"

"I beg your pardon?"

Apple cleared his throat of shrillness. He asked, "You think I should use my car on this mission?"

"I am telling you to do precisely that," Angus Watkin said. "A spot of stage-dressing is required here, and I have been informed that your vehicle is quite—ah—noticeable."

"A trifle bold, sir, yes."

"With private transportation like that, Porter, only the obtuse or the extra-clever would suspect you of being in the espionage business."

Apple began to nod slowly. Watkin was right. Watkin was always right. Ethel was as far removed as you could get from the unobtrusive medium-size black car.

That, however, was not what caused Apple to go on nodding. He was affirming to himself the fact, the marvellous truth, that he and Ethel would be working together on a caper.

The afternoon passed as swiftly as treacle through a straw. Apple paced, smoked and snacked. He failed at a siesta, succeeded in giving himself a headache—which he cured by lying on the couch with his feet in the air. The resulting pins and needles in one leg he cured by doing knee-bends.

Practising picking the pockets of an overcoat was a good and useful way of killing time, Apple found. Another was starting an expense account for this operation, which consisted of itemising with costs a pair of sun-glasses, one meat pie and a mug of soup.

A third time-killer came for Apple when he put

through a call to his superior at the United Kingdom Philological Institute.

Professor Warden, old and frail, possessed fourteen foreign languages, though he often had difficulty with the simpler words in English. A man who generated bewilderment, he smoked a pipe whenever he could find it.

"Yes, my boy," Professor Warden said when Apple had made the connection. "I'm free. Come along to my office."

"I'm not in the institute, Professor. I'm telephoning from home."

"Really? I hope you're not—um—"

"Resigning?"

"No, Porter. Infirm. Indisposed. Valetudinary. Something of that nature."

"No, I'm not," Apple said. "It's just that I work better at home when I'm preparing a lecture. At the institute I find it difficult to—er—"

Professor Warden suggested, "Cogitate? Ponder? Cerebrate? Excogitate? Lucubrate?"

"Yes, sir. Think."

"Which you need to do for your talk on Manx, naturally," the old man said. He went straight from that into a summary of the grammatical structure of the dying language. When he interrupted himself to ask Apple if he had seen his matches anywhere around, Apple got to the matter of absence from work. It was agreed that he would stay away until the lecture had been composed.

As a final killer of time, Apple walked across to Kensington to collect his car. He drove Ethel into Soho, where he started looking for a place to park, circling. He saw no empty parking slots.

Apple was beginning to get nervous when, at five

minutes to six, he passed the cafeteria for the second time and saw Sylvia. She was standing by the entrance.

Apple squealed to a stop, causing a honk from a truck behind. Smiling, Sylvia looked at the ex-taxi. As she saw its driver, her smile turned higher at one side.

Apple called out, "Hi. I'll be back as soon as I get a parking place."

Sylvia came trotting across. "They're not easy to find here at this time of day." The truck behind honked. "Is this beautiful thing yours?" She touched the paintwork with a gloved finger.

"Yes," Apple said softly, almost blushing with pleasure, "she is."

"Well, Russ, it's a delight to the eye."

"Thank you, Sylvia."

"There's hope for the English yet."

Apple said, "Look, you might as well get in, go with me while I try to find somewhere to park."

"Neat," Sylvia said. She opened the passenger door and got inside, pulled down one of the folding seats and sat behind Apple, who drove on as the truck honked again.

Sliding back the glass panel Sylvia said, "Since we're in the car, we might as well go somewhere else."

"You don't like the Circus pitch?"

"Not so much at night. I don't know why."

Apple suggested craftily, "Perhaps because it gets windy down there."

"You do get some pretty cold blasts," Sylvia said. "So where shall we go?"

Nodding with a satisfaction which he didn't find particularly satisfying, Apple said he would leave the choice up to her. She said the reverse of that. They decided after some debate that the non-chooser would be whoever was the first to see a dog.

On turning into Charing Cross Road, Apple saw a woman with a poodle. He called, "Snap!" Sylvia said all right, they would go to Waterloo Station. Apple wondered if she had seen the dog first.

During their ride to the major rail terminus, Apple answered Sylvia's questions about Ethel while glancing in the rear-view mirror for signs of Ned. He saw nothing, but kept his speed to the minimum so as to give no problems to a tail car.

Waterloo was crowded and noisy. In addition to the leaving commuters and arriving theatre-goers, there were groups of lost-looking tourists and a large troop of boy scouts complete with trumpeter. A cracked Last Post was being delivered to the edges of teeth as Apple and Sylvia ambled through the crowd.

Without moving his head too obviously, Apple looked around for Ned. His eyes switched back and forth like an auctioneer's. He was glad of his height. In fact, right now he wouldn't have minded being eight feet tall.

Sylvia said, "There he is."

Apple jerked out, "What?"

"That prime mark we all look for, Russ. Guy over there with the plaid cap. See? I'd say he's had a very good day at the races."

In trying to pin-point the man she meant, Apple, with relief, saw Ned. He said quickly, "There's a better one. I'll take him." He moved away. "Don't get lost."

Sylvia had no such intentions, Apple saw on glancing back when he was half-way to where Ned was gazing at a cigarette machine. She was two steps to his rear.

If she was that close at the moment of truth, Apple

reasoned, she would see his lack of skill, and it would be worse if Ned simply slipped him a wallet.

Quickening his pace to a stride, Apple made a detour. He went around the boy scouts, who were snarling at their trumpeter, cut in front of a moving luggage trolley and, coughing loudly, covered the final yards.

Ned glanced back. After catching his eye, Apple did the same. Sylvia was safely at a distance. She looked to be in no special hurry.

Apple went around in front of and close to the gaudily dressed expert in the art of help-yourself. He, accommodatingly, was holding forward one side of his striped jacket.

The inside pocket gaped. Apple thrust his hand in. He grasped a wallet and tugged.

Ned was snapped forward off balance. He closed his eyes, whined, and recovered by pushing against Apple. There was a furtive jumble of arms before Apple, with a gentler movement, was able to withdraw his hand.

"Thanks," he mumbled, convict-fashion, putting the wallet in his pocket as he slipped past. "Goodbye."

Ned whispered, "Promise me you really mean it."

Apple went over to Sylvia, who turned and walked along at his side, the comfort of which he found pleasing. She asked a casual, "Score?"

"Yes. Feels a fat one. Let's have a gander."

They went to the rear of a bookstall. Apple brought out the wallet and flipped it open. He extracted the money—eight five-pound notes plus a single—and said, "Could be better."

"Mustn't grumble," Sylvia said. "Forty-one quid isn't to be sneezed at." Then she grabbed his arm and hissed, "There!"

"Eh?"

"The prime mark. We've got to have him. Come on. I'll jostle and you dip."

She had moved away before Apple could speak. But he was trying as he sluggishly followed, his mouth working like a loose chew.

Ending that, accepting as hopeless the idea of wriggling out of the game, Apple eyed the man whose pocket he was supposed to pick, and who would, therefore, be the cause of the end of a blooming male-female relationship and of an intriguing mission.

But Apple told himself he would have to try. With a large amount of luck he might pull it off.

The man wore a grey raincoat, a disappointment after the colourful plaid cap. Fortyish, he had a cheery beery face and did indeed look as though he were on his way home from betting on winners.

With only a few feet and two intervening people to go, Apple realised that the prime mark could be a phony. If Sylvia was a Sickle, he was more than likely to be. The KGB would consider the possibility of Russ being a Brit, anticipate a set-up, and use a set-up of their own to get firm proof on his claim to be a pro pickpocket.

The way was clear, the mark was directly ahead. Apple had caught up to Sylvia. He was right at her shoulder as she now passed close to the left side of the man. She swayed, bumping against him.

At almost the same moment, Apple was about to pass on the right. He flipped a hand up by the man's chest—and gave in on the attempt as an impossibility. In any case, he was already going past.

Sylvia was moving ahead. Back to sluggish, Apple followed. Furiously, he tried to think of an excuse to explain his lack of success. He failed.

Oh well, Apple thought sadly. It was a fun little operation while it lasted.

Someone pushed up close beside him, coming from behind. He glanced down. The someone, he saw, was Ned, and although he didn't feel a thing, he understood when the expert muttered, "It's all yours, Ned."

"Thanks, Ned."

They branched away from each other. Apple, pressing his wrist against the new lump in his pocket, headed for where Sylvia dawdled.

Apple gave Ned 11 out of 10 for presence of mind. He had obviously sized up the situation and decided to do something about it. The only problem was, if the mark was a KGB arrangement, would he be aware of which man had dipped him?

Sylvia had her eyebrows raised in a question. Reaching her, Apple said nonchalantly, "Yes, I scored."

The restaurant, in Lambeth, would never make the guide books, even as a one-star tryer. The linen had too many patches, the menu was limited, and some of the mismatched cutlery bore the insignia of Cunard or British Rail.

Apple, however, patronised the Bread & Water occasionally because it was reliable. You knew the food would be stodgy, and it always was. Reliable.

But tonight Apple had come for the atmosphere. It was genuinely romantic, created by old dark wood on both low ceiling and walls, venerable Mantovani tapes played softly, and the oil lamps which had been in use ever since the power was cut off for non-payment of bills.

As the waiter slouched away after serving the mock pea soup, Sylvia picked up her spoon and said, "Go on, Russ, about that marvellous car of yours."

Apple shrugged. "Not much left. When I'd bought her from the cabbie who was retiring, I rented a spray machine and gave her a colour face-lift."

"And a fantastic job you made of it."

"Thanks," Apple said. He leaned forward. "I'll let you in on a secret, if you like."

Sylvia widened her blue eyes. "I love secrets."

"She has a name."

"Really?"

"Yes," Apple said, still in the clutch of invention. "I call her Geraldine." Anything would do so long as it wasn't Ethel, by which name, during her days with the Secret Services, she had become known to every spook in the West.

Thoughtfully, Sylvia said, "Yes, she has a definite Geraldine look about her."

"She was called something else before, but I changed it, which I think is fair enough. I did that with myself, after all. I switched to using my middle name, Russell, instead of my first, which doesn't appeal to me." He smiled in defence. "It's Appleton."

"Oh, that's not too bad," Sylvia said, still thoughtful. "Don't let your soup get luker."

See how simple that was? Apple mused. Just as easy as that other business at the station.

After they had looked at the mark's wallet (Sylvia closely), and tutted at the poor take (four singles), which Apple said he would leave there because such a sum was beneath his professional dignity (Sylvia blinking), they strolled to a mailbox so that Apple could get rid of the two wallets.

There, he had plunged with, "Look, Sylvia, I didn't really meet you tonight to have a busman's holiday. What I had in mind was dinner in an intimate setting. Mmm?"

"Lovely," Sylvia had said. She said it again now as she finished her soup.

Over the roast beef with Lancashire pudding, Apple talked about the United Kingdom Philological Institute. He made his job sound lowly, his talents as a linguist second-rate, his wage a pittance.

"At the moment," he said, "I'm doing the research for someone who's writing about the Manx language."

"What part of the world is that?"

"The Isle of Man. Out of a population of sixty-two thousand, only some three hundred can speak Manx."

"Fascinating," Sylvia told a forkful of cabbage. "But your job can't leave you much time for your other trade."

"It's only part-time. I quit the institute at noon."

"Good. We must go dipping together again sometime."

"Sure," Apple said. He poured more wine, giving the bottle that little twist when the glass was topped so there would be no dribbles. It was his sole piece of knowledge in connection with wines.

"On the subject of languages," Sylvia said. "I had three years of French at school, and now I don't remember more than a couple of dozen words. It's disgraceful."

"The school was in Sydney?"

"Melbourne." She went on to talk of her school-days, with affection and amusement. At one point she laughed warmly, showing a silver filling in an upper molar.

Apple noted that. Silver, he knew, was used extensively in Iron Curtain dentistry, even on the front teeth. He reasoned, however, that the KGB would have taken this known fact into consideration, and wouldn't have sent an agent into the field bearing such a give-away sign.

Nor, Apple mused, would Sylvia land herself with a background that could be so easily verified, if she were a

Sickle. While her name would no doubt check out at the school, a confrontation with other ex-pupils could quickly prove her a liar.

However, Apple realised, these things took time, and this appeared to be a short-term operation. So it didn't matter about perfection of cover, or if the prime mark was or was not a Hammer, or if Sylvia seemed not to know to what part of the world belonged Manx (no rarity that). Many of these factors could, in any case, be examples of KGB cleverness, allayers of suspicion.

Apple ended his mulling with the admission that, as he was decidedly smitten, he was the last person in the world to try to make an objective judgement. He would have to wait for strong evidence.

Conversation wandered until they were finishing their suet pud with custard, when Sylvia asked, "Have you been in the trade long, Russ?"

"Donkey's years. Since I was a teenager. And I've never had my collar felt."

"No, I've never been arrested either. We're lucky."

"And professional."

Dabbing her lips with a napkin that was two shades less white than her gloves, Sylvia said, "So, of course, you know a lot of people in our line of work."

"Loads and loads," Apple said expansively.

"In the West End?"

"All over the place." Seeing that Sylvia looked impressed, he bragged on, telling of all the sterling characters he counted as friends among the more refined levels of the criminal world of London.

"The only people I avoid," he said, "are those who go in for violence."

"I'm with you there, Russ. I'm quite a snob myself. After all, there are thieves and thieves."

"Indeed there are."

The waiter came to take plates. He left with non-acceptances to his threat of coffee.

Sylvia, leaning folded arms on the table, said in earnest, "This is wonderful, finding someone like you."

Apple, delighted, smiled bashfully. "Oh well."

"You knowing lots of bent people is perfect. You could be a great help to me."

Creakily: "Oh?"

"It's like this, Russ," Sylvia said. "I'd like to make a study of the London underworld, with the accent—naturally—on pickpockets, most of whom operate in the West End, where the crowds are thickest. I want to know how they got into the trade, and, oh, lots of other details. You understand?"

"Sort of."

"All I need to do is talk to these people. And that's where you can help me. I'd like you to introduce me to some of your friends." She smiled. "Will you?"

"Well, I—"

"Thank you, Russ. That's great. This study's something I've had vaguely in mind for ages, but it jelled a while ago when you talked about research into that language. So I have to thank you for that as well."

Apple could have kicked himself. He mumbled that it was a curious project for her to be interested in. Sylvia said it was actually her father's idea. A Londoner by birth, he had often talked of coming back and seeing how people in his profession lived and operated.

"I'd really be doing it for Dad."

"That's—um—very nice," Apple said, fumbling along while hoping to come up with a wriggle-out. "But . . ."

Sylvia reached across the table and pressed his hand. "But what, Russ?"

He found, "Well, it's autumn now, and many dips have gone abroad for the winter, to work in the sun."

Leaning back, Sylvia said briskly, "But I'm sure there'll still be oodles of them around. So how about tomorrow? We could meet when you get off work at midday. Is that all right with you? Oh, good. Honest, Russ, you're terrific. Really tops." She raised her glass high. "Let's drink to a successful relationship."

"Yes," Apple said weakly. "Let's."

As he drove, with Sylvia lounging grandly on the back seat, Apple was remembering a friend of his at university. In order to write a thesis on the penal system, he had got himself arrested for being drunk. He had paid the fine next morning but had insulted the magistrate, who had given him thirty days for contempt of court.

Sociologists were, in fact, noted for the extremes to which they were prepared to go in order to collect material, Apple thought. It wasn't too wild a notion, therefore, the one of Sylvia making a study of the London underworld, for which she was passing as a pickpocket—perhaps even with the knowledge of the police. They had not, after all, been consulted by Angus Watkin.

Apple clung to the idea because for one thing he liked it, for another it kept him from thinking about what was expected of him tomorrow afternoon.

Soon they came into Earl's Court, also known as Kangaroo Valley because of its high incidence of Australians. Apple, following directions from his passenger, stopped in front of a typical Victorian town house complete with pillared portico. A board with names and bell-buttons showed that the house had been divided into flats.

Jumping out smartly, Apple opened the rear door. He

bowed as Sylvia alighted, tugged an imaginary forelock when she handed him an imaginary tip.

They laughed. Using a bad accent, Apple said in French that he hoped the long journey hadn't been too arduous.

Sylvia said, "That's something respectable, I trust, my good man."

"Oh, absolutely."

She put out her hand. "Good night, Russ. Thanks for a fun evening. Shall we say one o'clock at that same place, the cafeteria?"

"Well, yes, okay," Apple said as limply as the hand-shake he gave. "Good night."

One minute later he was driving away, another five and he was inside a public telephone-box. He coined the slot and dialled. To the answering voice he gave two sets of digits.

After a pause, the man at the other end said, "You have the wrong number." Which meant that Angus Watkin was not available.

"This is a zero-three," Apple said crisply. He had always wanted the opportunity to use the minor emer-gency code (knowing somehow that he would never be in a position to use the major, nor yet the medium), so he said it again.

"I got you the first time," the man droned.

"I just wanted to be sure."

"I'll tape your problem and see to it that God hears. Go ahead. You're on."

Apple began with the rendezvous in Soho, ended with the handshake in Earl's Court. He left nothing out except the fact that he was forming a strong romantic attachment for the mystery girl.

The man grumbled, "That doesn't sound like a small panic station to me."

Sour sod, Apple thought. But next he felt a stab of compassion for the desk-pilot, who would no doubt give an elbow to be out in the field. He said, "I'm not a seasoned pro like you. I'm worried about the deal tomorrow. I need advice on how to get out of this one."

With less drone in his voice, the man said, "Okay, I'll push it along. You'll probably hear from God in the morning. Good night."

Apple headed for Bloomsbury. He felt fairly confident that Angus (God) Watkin would come up with a solution that was acceptable/believable to Sylvia, but hoped it wouldn't be something along the lines of a broken leg for the underling. Watkin, Apple knew, was capable of anything.

The underground garage was two streets away from Harlequin Mansions. After leaving Ethel there with a good-night pat, Apple went up to the street, where patches of autumn mist lurked like ghosts of the killer fogs of yester-year.

Although traffic passed sparsely, there were no pedestrians to be seen. Heard, yes. Footfalls sounded from somewhere behind Apple as he walked. He didn't make a test by stopping because they might have kept on, thus destroying the possibility that he was the hounds' hare. He was determined to make the emotional most of this mission.

At home Apple went straight to bed, straight to sleep, and straight into a dream. In it he was picking Sylvia's pockets. They were located on unusual and interesting parts of her skin-tight dress.

Awake at eight, Apple got up and put on his robe. This garment, a compensation for the drab clothes he normally wore, had a tartan pattern whose blocks were a foot square and whose hysterical greens, reds and yellows would have made the most boorish of artists whimper. It was not so much a design, more a mad scheme.

With his eye-opener coffee, Apple sat at the typewriter. Pecking to make the act last, he added to his expense account the Bread & Water bill and an estimate of the petrol used by Ethel. He thought it decent of him not to charge for wear on the tyres.

Apple was on his way to the kitchen, his mind planning an elaborate breakfast, when the telephone shrilled. He loped to the corner.

It was a bright voice that spoke, not the expected dull one owned by Angus Watkin. "Good morning," the man said. He quoted Apple's Service number. "Can you be downstairs in fifteen minutes? Old blue Morris, yours truly with a red scarf. We're going for a drive here and there."

Twelve minutes later, dressed, still chewing the slice of dry bread he had crammed in his mouth, Apple went below and out to the street. The blue Morris stood nearby, at its steering-wheel a man in his mid-twenties. Above the scarf was a pink face with the amused expression of a choirboy on the back row.

Apple got in. He exchanged casual greetings with the driver, who then drove off with, "I'm going to show you six set-ups. More are being readied in case they're needed."

"I'm not with you."

"The set-ups are places where you can take the young lady. Places where she will find what represents itself to be a pickpocket."

Apple nodded, smiling. "That's useful."

"Control says that you will explain to the lady that the

reason you are not taking her to dipping areas is because the dips don't like that kind of thing—socialising on the job. It happens to be true."

"Really?"

"Most don't even acknowledge each other's presence when they're working."

"You must've picked up that bit of info from Ned."

"Who?" the man asked with the blankness of a lie—and Apple was irked with himself for the unnecessary naming of names, for his amateurish slip, especially as the driver was younger than himself.

"No," the man said, "I picked it up on a course on dipping I took at Damian House."

Apple noted how old the man's voice sounded while musing that it must be pleasant to be able to retain facts that were actually useful to you.

Mumbling slightly, Apple said, "I wasn't feeling well when they ran that particular course during my training days at Damian House."

The driver said, "Control also wants it impressed upon you that you must lose no time in reaching your goal."

"My goal?"

"That, it would appear, is discovering what the lady's game is."

Apple nodded. "The chief's not available, I imagine."

"Right. Otherwise engaged."

Apple told himself it was foolish of him to feel slighted. And he felt that way because Angus Watkin wasn't solely concerned with and consumed by the Mysterious Affair of the Dubious Dip. It was hardly likely that this was the only caper he was running.

"Here's the first call," the driver said, steering the car into a mews.

Apple looked at him closely for the first time. Now he could see that the facial skin owed its pinkness and fresh youthfulness to the fact of being a graft.

Apple next noted, relevantly, that the neck which was mostly hidden by the red scarf had a dark, saggy, middle-aged appearance.

Apple felt chilled. This was due not so much to the question of what espionage misadventure had necessitated plastic surgery, but to the possibility that the man could have been a three-star agent who was nowadays reduced to the playing of minor roles.

"I'll introduce you," the driver said, "and then we'll shoot on to the next call."

Humbly, Apple said, "Thank you."

THREE

To be late for an appointment, in Apple's social ethos, was the height of offensiveness. The subtle statement to the met read: you are not important enough for me to take the little trouble needed to be on time. When romance entered the picture, and when that picture was framed by espionage, Apple took even greater care to be prompt if not early.

He had ten minutes to spare by the time he had found a place to park in Soho. Strolling, he headed towards the pavement rendezvous.

On turning the last corner, Apple saw that Sylvia had already arrived outside the cafeteria. Everything she wore, including a bag with a shoulder-strap, but excluding her white gloves, was in some shade of blue.

Apple saw next that Sylvia was talking to a man.

Quickly, Apple moved to the wall, where he stopped. There being many pedestrians on the narrow street, he felt he wouldn't be noticed by Sylvia.

She was listening with a frown to the stranger, who was young, good-looking and smartly dressed, which factors seemed at odds with his manner. It was lightly ingratiating. Apple made no mental comment on the situation.

Sylvia shook her head. She went on doing so as the man continued to talk, smiling, nodding, gesturing. He was like a salesman apologising by mien for the lies he nevertheless went on telling.

At last, with a shrug, Sylvia stepped back and turned away. The man's smile faded. After hesitating, he moved off. He came in this direction. Apple took several steps sideways and went into a shop doorway.

He had a fast debate with himself. Should he or should he not follow the stranger and risk being late for his date? The argument was becoming complicated by personal and professional needs when the man walked past the shop.

Feeling jangled and neurotic, Apple came out and followed. The need to play spy had won.

He stayed well back over the next few minutes as his hare went along several of the short streets. Knowing that, if he were an operative, the man might sense that he was being watched, Apple kept him in the periphery of his vision.

Finally, on the edge of Soho, the stranger stopped by a car. A large black Chevrolet, it had fixed to the bumper a circular plate bearing the initials CD—*corps diplomatique*. Apple was still memorising the licence number when the stranger drove away.

Running, Apple made his way back. The only thing he knew for sure was that the man couldn't be a member of the KGB, if, that is, Sylvia was Russian herself. He wouldn't be so stupid as to have been at the place where she was due to meet another party.

Apple maintained his run until he reached where Sylvia stood. Panting, he told her about the traffic jam that had delayed him.

Sylvia seemed complimented by his concern, and not at all suspicious when next he gasped an explanation of why they weren't going to see pickpockets in work areas.

As they were walking toward where he had left

Ethel, Sylvia said, "I had a funny experience while I was waiting, Russ. Flattering too, I guess."

"What happened?"

"A man tried to pick me up. He came on with that old haven't-we-met-before routine. He was good with it, but it still grew as high as an elephant's eye. I gave him the brush."

"Awful to look at, I suppose."

"Oh no, not at all," Sylvia said. "The opposite." She gave an accurate description.

"Some foreign Romeo, no doubt."

"British, Russ. No question of that."

Could be, Apple thought. Could be that everything about this thing was straight except for the CD plate, which some people used illegally to avoid parking tickets. And with Sylvia telling honestly of the man, that could mean she was straight as well.

Apple said, "Well, you can't blame the guy. It's your own fault for being so attractive."

Sylvia laughed. "Thank you, sir."

Later, as they were crossing Oxford Street in Ethel, Sylvia asked Apple about his work schedule. Was it every single afternoon? Did he always use the same areas?

"For instance, do you do the Circus on Mondays, Leicester Square on Tuesdays, and so forth?"

"No, I never follow patterns," Apple said. "They trip you up in the long run."

After that, in answer to further queries on the same theme, he gave safer, less positive answers. He thought he would be glad when he knew for sure the answer to the sonnet's question, "Who is Sylvia, what is she?"

In the mews, Apple parked and took Sylvia to the cottage with plastic roses around the door. He thumped hard on the wood, saying, "Joe's a little deaf."

The man who let them in was thin, with cheekbones like tongues in cheeks. He wore a sweater that reached down to his knees and his hair was messy. The image suggested a poet more than a petty criminal.

Introduction over, the faceless one called Joe took his visitors into a cluttered room. During the making and drinking of tea, he and Sylvia talked. It was an untidy conversation. The pretend deafness made it difficult for Sylvia with her questions, easy for Joe with his answers. He could choose what not to hear or what to misinterpret.

Saying he was going to check on their next visit, Apple excused himself and went upstairs to the telephone. He called in. To the voice at the other end he gave the Chevrolet's licence number and asked for a trace on ownership. The man told him to call back in half an hour.

Downstairs again, Apple sat out the rest of the bedraggled talk of methods and patterns. He didn't listen. He thought over the neatness of Angus Watkin's arrangement.

If Sylvia should come back to this place or the others, alone, she would find the genuine resident (an Intelligence affiliate), who would say that the supposed pickpocket was out and ask Sylvia to return later. The dip would be contacted and told to attend.

When Apple sloped his head in a let's-go, Sylvia responded with alacrity. It appeared as though she was more bored than frustrated.

The next call was a pub. It was crowded and noisy. The contact, Samuel, sat reading a newspaper, sharing a table with a young, hand-holding couple. He was old and stout and prosperous-looking, like a bishop resting on the seventh day from his vicar's labours.

As Apple and Sylvia approached, the couple got up to

leave—according to plan, Apple realised, having been there merely to keep the seats from being taken.

Apple introduced Sylvia. Again, as with Joe, she apologised for not removing her gloves to shake hands. Samuel called to a waiter; and then twice more as his call was drowned by the hubbub of talk.

They got served and Sylvia began with, "Why aren't you working today, Samuel?"

He bent closer. "What's that?"

Communication was better than with Joe, but only enough so to allay suspicion. It was still heavy going for Sylvia. This Samuel lightened with witty answers, some of which were even apropos of the questions. Sylvia began to smile.

Apple suggested they have the pub grub, a one-plate special. Samuel declined. Sylvia accepted, as long as it could be her treat. Apple gave in, but thought that it didn't bode well for the romance department, Sylvia's independence.

After their cottage pie, Apple took the plates back to the bar. Unseen from the table, he slipped into a hallway and found a telephone. He called in. The man on duty told him, "The car is the property of the Israeli Embassy."

They came out of the pub onto the wide avenue. Traffic was sporadic and leisurely. There were few pedestrians. In scanning about while performing a stretch of his arms, Apple saw no one suspicious. He wondered just how many spies were playing in this game.

"What a character that Samuel is," Sylvia said. "He really slays me."

"Did you pick up anything useful for your study?"

"Not much, Russ. But I mustn't be impatient."

"Come on," Apple said. "Ethel's over there."

Sylvia looked up at him. "Who?"

Apple caught his breath, tensing at the mistake. That was bad enough, but now he could feel a blush prickling its way up his chest.

"That woman across the road," he said, confusedly pointing in the direction of an old man. "I—um—knew her years ago. She used to—"

Apple broke off at the sound of footfalls. They were coming from behind and as rapid as high-speed clapping. By the time Apple had swung around to place the source, the runner was almost here.

He was youthful and tall, with long hair that swam out behind like ribbons from a fan. He wore jeans and a tight black sweater. His features were set.

The runner flashed by, right beside Sylvia, who jerked out, "Hey!"

For a moment Apple thought that she had been hit by the man; his mind was more concerned with the pleasant fact that his blush hadn't advanced. Then he saw that the runner, who was already several yards ahead, was holding a blue bag. It had been snatched off Sylvia's shoulder.

"Stop!" Apple shouted, lurching forward. "Thief!"

He ran. Within three seconds he was moving at his fastest, which was fast. To begin with, his legs were long; to end with, he had once been trained for a caper in the skills of running.

The man glanced back, raced on. He had no style but there was youth on his team. Also, he was shrewd: when a street-sweeper ahead looked at him closely, he yelled, "Stop that man!"

Apple was gaining rapidly. His legs were fine and his mind was cool. In between, however, there was his stomach. It began to protest at the action when it was trying to give a welcome to a large helping of cottage pie plus two sherries on the rocks.

Yet he went on gaining. As he passed the sweeper, he was only two yards behind the runner. He could hear Sylvia shouting encouragement.

The trick tried by the runner was an old one; Apple had used it himself. Therefore he was prepared when the man in front suddenly dropped to all fours. Instead of tripping over him, Apple leapt.

Leapt, and turned immediately on landing. He was back before the runner had reached his full height. He grabbed his arm.

"Got you," Apple said in a combination gasp and belch. His stomach was in a quiet rage.

There followed a brief skirmish of twisting and tugging. Then, from his hip-pocket, the man whipped out a cosh. He brought it down heavily on the capturing hand.

With a yell of pain, Apple let go. At once the man ran off, and, in the surge of leaving, lost his hold on Sylvia's bag. It fell to the ground. The man almost stopped, looking behind, but then ran on.

Apple was relieved that he need do no more running: his stomach had a steady fume going. In any case, he wasn't interested in making a citizen's arrest. On a mission, you stayed clear of involvements.

A motor cycle came roaring along. It slowed when level with the runner, who charged into the roadway and to the bike. He got onto the pillion behind another long-haired man. The motor cycle roared away.

Apple walked back to meet Sylvia, who was coming at an urgent stride. His damaged hand he held in a dangle, where it throbbed painfully.

Rather than be shaken by the incident, however, Apple was pleased. It had served him well. The Ethel mistake was no longer in the air, his resulting blush had been killed, and not only had he been able to play Rescuing Knight to Sylvia's Maiden-in-Distress, but he had sustained an injury in the cause.

There was a ten-minute confusion of inquest, advice and condemnation of modern youth, in which joined the street-sweeper, several people from nearby houses and a sway of customers from the pub. Apple was the least animated. He glowed calmly, belching, in response to Sylvia's thanks and praise and solicitous attention.

She insisted on a doctor. They were directed to one farther along the street. He said no bones were broken and it was time the government brought back flogging. Apple mentioned that it was still on the books in the Isle of Man.

Outside again, holding his red, swollen hand where it wouldn't be forgotten, Apple said, "Right, let's get on to the next stop."

Sylvia shook her head. "No, Russ, you should go home and lie down. You look quite pale. I'll get a cab so you won't have to use that hand so much, driving me back to my place."

Pale was how Apple felt, physically, with the cottage-pie stomach and sherry-flavoured belches. So he didn't insist. It was agreed that he would pick Sylvia up in Earl's Court at six o'clock.

After seeing her into a cab, Apple drove one-handedly home. Smiling, he relived the look of concern and admiration in Sylvia's blue eyes. But he was also forced to admit to the fact that he sensed in her a certain reserve, as though she hadn't fully accepted him yet. Could there be a boy-friend lurking in the background.

At the flat Apple soaked his hand in cold water with

ice-cubes, afterwards applying an extra-tight bandage. He felt vaguely noble.

Belching his way to the bedroom, he lay down, at which point the telephone rang. The mysterious Sylvia, Apple thought, getting up smartly. She would be checking to see that he got home all right.

In his living-room Apple lifted the receiver and heard, "Were you asleep, Porter?"

"No, sir. I was doing my expense account."

"Honestly, of course," Angus Watkin murmured.

"Yes, sir," Apple said. "Which reminds me. What am I supposed to do with the forty-one pounds that was in the wallet I lifted from Ned?"

"Spend it, Porter, itemising as you go. Then you'll have less trouble getting the remainder of your expenses back from Accounts. That department parts with small sums of money readily enough, I'm told."

"Very good, sir."

Angus Watkin said, "Now I want your progress report. You may proceed."

Apple was aware as he talked that his report had little in it of progress—at least, in respect of finding out what Sylvia was up to. Because of that, he made a lot out of the stranger who had tried to pick her up.

"Yes," Angus Watkin said, "I heard of your request about a car's ownership."

"Does this mean, sir, that the Israelis are trying to get in on the act, as well as the CIA?"

"That would appear to be the case, Porter. And that would rather indicate the need for haste on your part, would it not?"

"Yes, sir, it would," Apple said. "I'm trying my best."
Not waiting to hear his Control's sigh, he carried straight

on with a crisp, "Additionally, there was the incident of the snatched bag."

"True."

"It's quite possible for the pair to have been ordinary thieves, I know," Apple said, not believing that for a moment. "I can't help thinking, however, that there might be something else to it."

From the other end of the line, a silence. It ended with Angus Watkin saying heavily, "I had expected you, Porter, to realise at once what that little bit of business was all about. Realise, and be appreciative."

"I don't understand, sir. Appreciate what?"

"The fact that you no longer have to worry about going out pickpocketing with the young lady. You couldn't, could you, not with a damaged hand?"

So the bag-snatching pair were Watkin people, Apple mused as he lay on his bed. True, it ought to have been seen at the time. A real snatching team would have had the motor cycle there immediately; in this case the getaway had to wait until the hand had been hit.

But it had been an excellent, realistic job, Apple allowed. One, furthermore, that had to be done with Sylvia as a witness. She had to see it rather than be told, than have him fake a battered hand. That might have come unstuck, his using the hand in reacting spontaneously to something, maybe something created by Sylvia as a test.

But was Sylvia suspicious? Apple wondered. Had it been doubt or real concern that had made her insist on a doctor, and stay close during the examination?

Apple didn't know the answer any more than he knew if the damage, which wasn't overly vital, represented Angus Watkin's revenge for underling Appleton Porter having dared to interfere in a mission.

Apple slept.

Up at five o'clock, he fixed himself coffee. Leaving the spoon in his cup for the devil-may-care of it, he went to his typewriter. He started a new list of expenses, deducting each item from the forty-one pounds. His task was stretched out pleasingly by the fact of his typing with the forefinger of the left hand. That his right hand had stopped hurting he managed to ignore.

At one minute before the ten he had allowed himself to get to Sylvia's place, Apple left the apartment. At six o'clock promptly he parked in front of the Earl's Court house. He went up under the portico and rang Sylvia's bell. Her voice, wrapped in static, asked who it was.

"Me—Russ," Apple said. "Shall I come up?"

Quickly: "No, I'll be right down."

Apple turned away thoughtfully. Feeling unsure of himself, he went and leaned against Ethel.

On coming outside, Sylvia, her features bland, asked, "How's the damage?"

Apple showed his hand, which was noticeably swollen under its bandage. "A bit tender. I'll bet I could even dip with it, but I'm not going to take any stupid chances." He opened Ethel's rear door.

Not moving forward to enter, Sylvia said, "I went dipping myself this afternoon."

"Oh yes?" Apple asked in a casual tone, but he didn't like Sylvia's attitude.

"Piccadilly. In the station. I didn't score, but a curious thing happened."

Again: "Oh yes?"

"A man came up and started to talk to me."

"You attract 'em like flies."

Sylvia shook her head. "No Romeo stuff. He was old enough to be dead."

"What, then?"

"A professional Nosy Parker, that's what he claimed to be. He said he'd been watching me for some time now and he knew I was a pickpocket."

Apple asked, "Blackmail?"

"No," Sylvia said. "The reverse. He was trying to do me a favour. He said he'd seen me with you, and that in his opinion you were a policeman."

Apple, startled, leaned away. Some seconds passed before he managed, "Me? A cop? Are you kidding?"

"That's what the man said."

"But you don't believe that, surely."

"I suppose it is possible."

Recovering, Apple said, "But if I were a cop I would've arrested you long ago. I had the evidence when you lifted my wallet. This is ridiculous."

"Well . . ."

"Although, I should be used to this kind of thing by now. It's not the first time I've had it. Being as tall as I am, it's inevitable. I've often been taken for a cop. It's insulting and annoying."

Her face less bland, Sylvia said, "I had to tell you about this, Russ."

Apple smiled. "Of course. But listen. I give you my word of honour, if that means anything, that I am not connected with the police in any way, manner or form, nor have I ever been, nor have I plans to be. Okay?"

"Okay," Sylvia said, answering the smile, though not too strongly. "Sorry about that."

"Forget it. Let's go and see my old pal Ned."

A moment later, driving, Apple was still uncomfortable. He knew that Sylvia's reserve had increased, which was bad both for their relationship and the mission. And as for the old man, could be he was all that he claimed, but most likely he was a foreign agent: he wanted the tall nuisance out of the Sylvia picture so that he could get one of his own team in.

The old man could also be a figment of Sylvia's imagination, Apple realised. She could have had doubts after the hand-bashing incident. Trouble was, there seemed no way of dispelling them.

After a short drive during which there was no conversation, they stopped across the road from a snack-bar. Through its large window Ned could be seen at a table. Wearing neither his bow-tie nor loud coat, but sombre clothes, he had the place almost to himself.

They went across the traffic-busy road and inside, where it was quiet. Ned played it affable. He shook Sylvia's hand with avuncular enthusiasm, ushered her into a chair, fetched tea and cakes for all of them, sat with every sign of enjoyment and said: "This is nice. I love to talk, and Russ here told me on the blower that you want me to talk about the old game of keeping a hand in. Nothing could suit me better. Since I retired, I've been bored stiff. As stiff as my arm gets with the bloody rheumatism. If it wasn't for that, I'd be out on the dip right this minute, at the races, maybe, or with the tourists outside Buckingham Palace, or working the early movie queues."

With surprise, Apple noted that instead of looking pleased (ambience peaceful, contact verbose), Sylvia appeared to be slightly disappointed. This showed in body language, the way she eased aside and folded her arms.

Apple told himself, however, that he could be wrong. He could be reading signs that weren't really there because of leaning over backwards not to lose sight of the mission, not be purblinded by his smittenship.

Ned talked. Sylvia listened, interjecting a question from time to time. Ned answered at garrulous length, continuing to present a picture of someone enjoying a rare treat.

After a while Apple noticed that, on the other side of the road, a man was showing great interest in Ethel. Short and dark and fortyish, wearing a shabby raincoat, the man stood gazing at the ex-taxi with his head on the move, shifting from one side to the other.

Although this sort of thing happened constantly, Apple never tired of watching Ethel-appreciators. There was, of course, always the occasional moron who laughed, but mostly the response was highly favourable, bred of awe, envy and admiration. What Apple enjoyed in particular was to stroll up to Ethel when she had drawn an audience and, yawning ostentatiously, slip into the driver's seat.

Which, Apple saw with a tightening of his spine and senses, was precisely what the dark man was doing now, though minus audience and yawn.

"Excuse me," Apple mumbled, rising.

As he walked out, he reflected that the man was sure to be merely a hard-faced bastard who wanted a closer examination. No thief with a brain in his head would steal a vehicle as outstanding as Ethel.

Outside on the kerb, held there by the bustling traffic, Apple wondered if he was being as naïve as he had over the bag-snatching. The man could be planting a bomb or trying to cripple the motor.

Apple began to stride swiftly back and forth, fuming at passing cars for the delay. It eased him only slightly to note that the dark man seemed to be doing nothing more amiss or dangerous than sitting with his rotten interloper hands on the steering-wheel.

A gap came in the traffic. Spurting, Apple went across the road. He stopped by the driver's window, which was rolled down, and asked, "What's all this about?" His tone he held as mild as his expression because, after all, the man might be an innocent who had been goaded into this intimacy by instant infatuation.

The man turned his head slowly. He looked to be totally unconcerned and uninvolved, as though he were sitting on a park bench, not in someone else's car.

He asked, "May I help you?"

Apple sighed. "Now listen," he began. The reason he didn't finish was because he sagged unconscious from the blow on the back of his head.

Boxers who have been knocked out invariably describe the experience in identical terms: the lights went off. There is no memory of punch or pain.

That's how it was with Apple when he came to, which, the transition to consciousness, happened rapidly, the minimum of time spent on passing through grogginess.

After blinking several times, Apple closed his eyes. This, along with keeping quite still, was as taught in Training Five. It was both to feel out the situation and to make sure that the body was in movable condition.

The latter Apple checked by tensing himself in one section after another. There were no wounds and nothing broken. He did, however, have a tenderness at the base of his skull. He assumed that he had been hit there by a projecting piece on a passing vehicle.

Throughout the foregoing, Apple had been sensing out his immediate surroundings. He was lying on his side, on something hard that vibrated. There were matching sounds. Obviously, he was on the floor of a van. He was being taken to hospital.

But, Apple thought, if he had been struck with the

force of a moving vehicle he would have pain as well as blood. There was only that dry tenderness.

Ergo: the blow had probably been delivered by a person, one who was an expert in rendering the victim insensate while causing minimal damage.

A male voice came from close at hand. It asked, "How's he doing?"

After a slight pause, another voice said, "Out like a dead donkey."

Both voices used the same language—Spanish.

"You're sure?"

"Listen to me. I know my job. Brother, when I hit 'em they stay hit."

Apple was grateful for the Latin machismo that made a person resist admission that whatever he did could be anything less than perfect.

The first voice said, "Not that he'd give us much of a problem anyway."

"This long strip of misery? Hell no."

To be sure, Apple kept his eyes closed. He thought about the accent. Even if Spanish hadn't been one of his stronger languages, he would have known that the men were South American, not from the Iberian Peninsula. The slur was unmistakable. But he would have to hear more in order to pinpoint the particular country.

Cautiously, Apple opened his eyes to a slit. The van, he saw, was old, its floor and wall bearing rust and scratches. A side door was of the rolling type.

Neat, Apple thought. A three-man job. One to draw their victim across the road, one to drive up with a van, one to knock the victim out and push him through the wide, sliding door.

Apple turned his head slowly. Now he felt pain in the tender spot behind his right ear. But it was light, acceptable. There had been worse pains on those mornings after a rash, four-sherry evening. He kept on turning his head until he had the front of the van in view.

The two men showed from the shoulders up above the shabby seat. Both were dark-haired. One, the passenger, had a large bald patch, so Apple guessed him to be the macho voice, and was proved right when now the man spoke: "You should've taken a left there."

The driver said, "One way's just the same as the other."

"What's that got to do with it? That's the way we chose."

"In fact, this way's half a minute quicker."

The balding man turned his head away. "You should've taken a left there."

Cuban, Apple decided firmly. Which meant that either friend Fidel was trying to pry a return favour out of Auntie Russia or had ideas of his own. If, that is, the pair were working for their homeland. They could be KGB, or almost anything else.

Apple didn't care especially. All he was interested in at the present was escape. He considered the possibilities.

First, the sliding door. It was sure to be unlocked. No time would have been available during the snatch for the men to start fiddling around with keys—if they had any: the van was sure to be stolen, its motor started by crossing the ignition wires.

Apple thought that all he need do, therefore, was wait until they were moving slowly or stopped at traffic lights, then yank back the door and throw himself out. If everything went well, the operation would take about three seconds. He could be off and running before the pair realised what had happened.

But, judging by body vibrations, they were going at a

good clip. Which, Apple reckoned, probably meant that they were on a high-speed throughway. The driver wouldn't otherwise risk being stopped by the police for speeding.

And time was of the essence. If they were gauging the journey in half-minutes, it had to be a short one. Escape at the destination might be impossible.

Apple remembered Ned. The dipping expert was sure to have seen the snatch and to have alerted Upstairs. The alarm would be out. There could be someone tailing the van right now, waiting for the right moment to intercept.

Still, Apple knew that in the spy game the only person you could rely on or trust completely was yourself. So he had to make his own try for freedom.

In case Macho looked around, Apple closed his eyes and turned his head to the side. In doing so, he realised that his legs were bent, his knees almost touching the seat back. His tallness had made that necessary.

Interesting, Apple thought. If, in one fast and smooth movement, he could roll onto his back, jack-knife his legs and then shoot them out high and apart, he might land a kick on the head of each man. Even if he were imprecise, the kicks glancing off, the shock would be enough. The driver would automatically brake, speed would be reduced, the escape door could be used.

Okay? Apple asked himself.

Okay, he answered. And do it now. One, two . . .

"It's that next corner," Macho said.

"I know, I know."

"Just telling you."

"How's the long one?"

After a pause: "Sleeping like a babe in the womb."

"A nice neat job we did."

"We?"

The exchange ending there, Apple thought tensely, One, two, three—*move!*

He flung himself over onto his back. At that same moment the van teetered severely—in taking a corner at speed, Apple realised as his roll was forced to continue. He crashed against the side.

Macho said, laughing, "It's not his day, is it?"

Where the van stopped, it was dim. Apple received this information via the lids of his closed eyes. He lay limp and untidy beside the wall of scarred metal.

The motor died, doors opened, the two men began to get out. The driver said, "It might be better to rope him."

"Why bother? He's not going anywhere."

The doors slammed shut. Apple stayed exactly as he was. He heard a jumble of footsteps, one heavy thud and then another. The dimness became full darkness in time with the second thud.

Silence.

Apple opened his eyes. He could see nothing. Cautiously he sat up. He got out his cigarette lighter and flicked it on. Moving in a squat, he went to the sliding door. When he tugged on it, it began to open, but made a loud squeak.

"Shhh," Apple said. He crouched up and got over onto the seat. The nearest door opening easily, quietly, he went out to the ground. Three feet away was a brick wall. Going back between it and the van, he came to a pair of doors—authors of those dark-making thuds.

He was in a regular house-type garage, Apple realised. And he knew that the house must be in a quiet area because there was nothing to be heard through the heavy wood. So, any untoward noise in here would be picked up by the pair of Cuban heels.

Apple circled his prison twice. There were no tools and nothing that could be used as an implement; nothing, in fact, that a private garage would normally have, except a ruptured tyre and a petrified paintbrush.

Back at the doors, Apple found they had no keyhole, no lock he might have been able to pick. Which meant that they were held either by a bar or a padlock.

Probably the former, Apple thought after pressing hard on the wood and getting only the slightest give. It couldn't have been worse.

Apple lit a cigarette. He gave his lighter a rest while he smoked and tried to come up with some brilliant method of escape using a has-been paintbrush and a dead tyre. He burned his fingers.

There was only one thing for it, Apple decided. He would have to try getting the van started, and, reversing it, break through the doors. But there were problems.

The motor was almost sure to be heard. The van had only three feet to travel, so wouldn't be able to build up speed. The noise of impact would certainly draw the Cubans' attention, if the motor hadn't.

But it was the only solution, Apple thought as he went back to the front of the van. And it might not be wise to stick around to see what developed.

He got in behind the steering-wheel. His lighter on, he saw that, as expected, the ignition was keyless and loose wires were dangling from underneath.

Apple reached up to a dome-light. It worked, bathing the interior with yellowness. Cheered, he put his lighter away and settled to the pairing of wires.

The first few tries produced nothing. Then a red bulb

came to life on the dashboard. Apple quickly twisted the raw wires together and pressed the starter.

There was a high-pitched whine. In the enclosed space, it sounded monstrously loud. Apple shook his head at it. He gasped as the motor caught, held his breath as it stumbled, gasped again when it began to run smoothly. The noise was lower than the starter.

Apple switched on the headlights. He hadn't done so earlier because that could have drained the battery. Brightness flooded the garage, thrown back from the wall ahead.

Apple slammed reverse gear into place and let out the clutch. The van jerked mightily without moving. The engine died. Apple realised that he had forgotten to release the hand-brake.

He did so now, growling at his stupidity. He restarted the motor. He revved fiercely and shot the van backwards. It hit the doors.

The crash was like a house falling. Apple's ears hurt. So did his chest—from his being thrown forward onto the wheel when the van halted.

The doors had held.

Apple slapped a change of gear and went forward. Not unusually for him, he went too far. He hit the wall and the headlights went out in a screech of shattering glass.

The dome-light still glowed. Apple could see to brutalise the gears. He reversed. There was another crash, another thud of chest on wheel, another failure to break out.

Apple was seized by a fit of coughing. Briefly, he thought it was because of those hits on the chest. Next, he understood that the garage was beginning to fill with lethal exhaust fumes.

With a deep breath he ended the coughing. He went

forward. Engaging reverse gear, he pulled on the parking brake and revved the motor while riding the clutch. The van trembled in its effort to move, which it did, speedily, when now Apple released the brake.

The crash was less, his chest didn't quite reach the steering-wheel. Another failure, he assumed. But it wasn't so. Though the locking device held, the hinges gave way.

The doors fell together like a drawbridge—and the van rolled over them into the stark daylight.

Apple braked. Flinging open the door he fell out, onto gravel. He took great gulps of clean air while looking swiftly all around. His tension eased.

The garage stood alone. On every side was parkland, grass dotted with trees and huge clumps of bushes. A gravel path ran into a copse, above which could be seen a roof-top.

Apple's tension came on full again as he heard voices. But there weren't only two and the language wasn't Spanish. It sounded like an English garden party when some clown spikes the tea with gin.

The babble, growing fast in volume, was coming from the direction of the building. Grinning with alarm, Apple began to back away. He had reached grass when the owners of the voices came into view on the path, hurrying.

There were forty to fifty people of both sexes, their faces alive with curiosity. Some wore white, some were in ordinary clothes, most wore dressing gowns. Half a dozen were in wheelchairs. Apple realised that he was on the grounds of a hospital.

He turned and ran.

By the time Apple found a telephone, at a service station, he had recovered from being chased by gleeful medics and invalids. Where it had no doubt been for that whooping group a nice break in the monotony of routine, for him it had been an unwanted, surrealistic experience, one coming right on top of the trauma and battering and gassing of escape. It had also had a farcical quality that he could quite do without.

Apple called in. To the answering voice he identified himself by number and said, "This is the all-clear. I'm out and about."

"Then we can call off the bloodhounds, eh, and send the cavalry home?"

"If it's not too much trouble."

The voice said, "I'll tape you for God. Go ahead."

Apple told the whole thing, leaving out only the surrealism, which, he knew, he would fail to make sound dramatic. He closed with his conviction that he hadn't been rumbled as a Brit, that the Cubans simply wanted him out of the way so someone else could move in on Sylvia, as with the old man who had fingered him as a cop.

"Okay," the officer on duty said. "Now let me fill you in on what we got from Ned. You have not, I take it, seen the lady yet."

"No, I haven't."

"Good. There's nothing like everyone telling the same story. Somehow, it seems to help."

"Somehow," Apple said, "I'm not terribly in the mood for whimsy. If you know what the word means."

Following a bleak pause, the man said, his voice with equal bleakness, "Ned saw the agent hit. A vehicle came alongside and took hitter and agent off. A third man, the bait, left on foot but soon changed to a car. Description of men and vehicles, including numbers, available. Interested?"

"No, thanks. I want to know about the lady."

"The lady presented a façade of bewilderment. Going back to her after tailing the bait, Ned told her he had no idea what it was all about, but that it was none of his business. They separated. End of report."

Contrite on account of his waspishness, Apple said, "Thank you. It was nicely concise."

The man grunted. He said, "So you can play it anyway you like about the snatch."

"Sure. Over and out, as the saying goes."

"So long. And one last word."

"What is it?"

"God's getting impatient."

From the service station Apple took a taxi to the area of the snack-bar. Ethel was waiting. A five-minute check of her pertinent sections showed that she hadn't been tampered with or booby-trapped.

Driving through the dusk, Apple wondered about a bewildered Sylvia. It was possible that she had been, but equally possible that she was in on the snatch, that the Cubans were on her team. The story had better be straight.

At the house in Earl's Court, when the squawk-box came alive, Apple blurted, "Are you all right?"

"Russ! It's you. What *happened?* And what d'you mean, am *I* all right?"

"I thought you might have been in trouble."

"Me? No, nothing. I saw this man . . ."

Apple heard most of it out before interrupting with, "Look, Sylvia, I can't talk to you through this bloody box."

"Okay. Hold on. I'll be right down."

Apple sighed. He went to Ethel and got in the back, leaving the door open. After ruffling his hair, he looked around for dirt that he could rub on his face. There was no dirt. He unravelled part of the bandage on his hand.

Sylvia came out and joined him with a flurry. She

seemed stimulated, concerned. Apple let her rewrap his bandage while he talked. He also slid his left arm along the seat back and oozed himself close.

The version he gave was of coming conscious to find himself in a van, inside a garage, and of breaking out. He made a short story long because Sylvia, finished with the hand, leaned back against his arm.

"How terrible," she said in a low voice. "What an incredible experience."

It was dark now, but illumination came and went from the headlights of passing cars. Apple felt cosy and romantic. He realised that the Cubans had probably done him a favour, that this could dispel any doubts Sylvia might have had over the hand-disabling incident. She seemed less reserved.

Letting his left hand slip down onto her shoulder, Apple said, "Yes, I wouldn't want to go through something like that again. I'm no hero."

"But what does it all mean, Russ?"

"I've puzzled my brains about it. All I can think of is that it's some gang. They're warning me off my regular dipping pitches, so their own people can have them to themselves. That's why I was worried about you."

"Oh dear," Sylvia said. "Gangsters I can do without. I'm not heroic either. Couldn't there be some other explanation?"

"Nothing else has occurred to me," Apple said. "Violence isn't something I'm familiar with." He snuggled his arm closer.

"No enemies?"

"Not a single one."

Sylvia asked, "So what, if anything, can you do?"

"Well, it might be an idea if I—if we both stayed out of circulation for a while. Or go to fresh fields."

"I don't mind not working for a few days. But you can still take me to see your dip friends, can't you?"

"Absolutely," Apple said. He told himself, Stop talking and kiss her, you ranting lunatic.

"Oh, terrific."

"I'll pick you up tomorrow about one o'clock, if that's all right with you."

"It's perfect, Russ."

Bravely, Apple said, "Just like you—perfect."

"That's sweet," Sylvia said softly. She turned and smiled up at him.

It was quite a long way to go, Apple realised as he began to lower his head. In fact, he thought, his neck might not bend that far down. Ought he to ease her sideways? No, better to shuffle lower in the seat.

Moving away, Sylvia said, "I have to go."

Apple craned his down-angled head. "Eh?"

"I need rest. I'm very shaken by the whole thing. You must be as well, of course. Far worse. Shattered. You've had a hell of a time, Russ."

"No, no, I'm fine, fine."

"You'll get a nervous reaction soon. Bound to, since you hate violence. I'm getting one myself. You should be resting in bed."

Apple straightened. "I think that what I really need is a nice cup of home-brewed tea."

Sylvia got out onto the kerb. Turning, she said, "That's an excellent idea, Russ."

"Yes?"

"Yes. When you get home, make yourself one before you go to bed."

The following moment, with a blown kiss, Sylvia was gone and Apple was thinking glumly, God isn't the only one who's getting impatient.

FOUR

Their first call next day was at a music store. The phony salesman, who had the place to himself, looked to be still in his teens. He had a punk haircut, with one level dyed orange, the other dyed blue. While he talked to Sylvia about his supposed extra-curricular work, picking pockets, he snapped his fingers and shimmied to the hi-fi music that was going at full blast.

Their second stop was a street corner. The suburban, traffic-free shopping area was peaceful and pleasant, with songbirds chirping in tame trees. The imitation pickpocket lounged on the corner like a post-war spiv who could sell you anything from ration books to a stolen shirt. He had greased-down hair, more padding in his shoulders than an American footballer, and a pencil-line moustache that was 90 per cent pencil. His attitude to Sylvia was flirtatious. Between giving skimpy answers to her questions, he was lavish with compliments, eye-rolls and lewd grins. He did everything except perform the gropes that his constantly moving hands were shaping. "It's time we were off," Apple kept saying, which wasn't part of the act.

Call number three was on a grumpy, middle-aged man who acted as though he were suspicious of Sylvia. He would tell her hardly anything. A nice reverse touch, Apple thought.

They broke for a late lunch. The food was fair and the wine tasted good enough to have known grapes. Over the final glass, when they were both pink of cheek, Apple again tried to pump Sylvia gently for information on herself. He got nowhere. He realised that although she might have accepted him for what he had represented himself to be, and might even have taken a liking to him, she was still sticking to her one-person game.

Dozy, they decided to continue the break with a visit to a cinema. As they settled in their seats, Apple had all manner of plans in mind. Next he knew, Sylvia was shaking him awake to the sound of last-fade music.

After coffee in a snack-bar, they went to a dismal little house in a terrace. It was fit only for mess-loving midgets with no sense of smell. Yet the occupiers were cheerful. They were a couple and three children. The baby yelled every time the nipple was taken away from its mouth, the toddlers ran around boisterously, the man and woman took turns in telling how they took turns in going out to pick pockets. The set-up was so natural that Apple could only assume that it was mostly genuine. He kept wondering how it could otherwise have been arranged, which prevented his threatening blush over the breast-feeding from coming to hot fruition.

The next visit was to a different world, an apartment in a high-rise building. They sat on a balcony overlooking the Thames at Tower Bridge, sipping champagne cocktails and listening to an elderly, cultured woman. She told the story of her professional life in the world's major cities. When she was asked by Sylvia if she ever worked railway stations, the woman looked offended. "Only hotels," she said. "Of the first category, of course." She didn't offer a second cocktail.

The old man was another switch. His apparent home was a shack in an East End junkyard, his clothes were a haven for orphan oil, his accent was mangled Middle European. During his rambling talk he took short runs in Polish, Russian, Czech and Magyar. He said he hadn't "vorked at da pickink of pockets" for over a month because business in the junk line had been good, at which point Sylvia made murmurs about moving on. The old man told her, in Russian, that she was about to get oil on one of her gloves. Unheedful, Sylvia put her hand on the glistening smear.

Five minutes later, driving, Apple began whistling. He didn't know if he was feeling the effects of lunch wine and balcony cocktail, or if he was buoyant over the now strong possibility that Sylvia was straight—on account of her non-response to the Russian.

She could have been acting, Apple knew, just as the old man could have been following Angus Watkin's orders in using the standard ploy, but it took a seasoned pro to get by it, and Sylvia was young.

Apropos of alcohol and old tricks, it occurred to Apple that he could try the *in-vino-veritas* routine, in earnest. A few tongue-looseners might work wonders.

Turning his head to the side he asked, "How about another break? Maybe a reviving drink?"

"Terrific idea, Russ," Sylvia said. She was rubbing with a tissue at the stain on her white glove. "And somewhere elegant, if you follow."

"I'm walking on your heels."

The hotel they went to was new and smart, expensive and fashionable. Its cocktail lounge, though crowded, had merely a hum of discreet conversation, as if everyone was afraid of not overhearing what others were saying. The waiters glided like statues on skates.

Apple and Sylvia soon got served at the table they had chosen in the centre of the lounge; sherry on the rocks and a dry martini. They sat relaxed, smoking, talking idly.

Apple decided he would wait until the next round before he started on a line of subtle questioning. Meanwhile, he needed to resolve the problem of how to get rid of part of his drinks so that he wouldn't get plastered himself.

By the time their waiter brought the third round, Apple had asked no questions and was still without a solution. He dropped his money twice in paying. Haughty, he told the waiter to keep the change. Sylvia giggled. Apple thought it crafty of him to have injected a bit of humour into the campaign.

He and Sylvia went on sipping and chatting, both with a little more fervour than before.

Apple was wondering if he should try the spilling gambit, in preference to the one which had just come to him—pouring the alcohol onto Sylvia's glove to remove the oil stain—when he saw a face he knew.

The man, neatly dressed, was fortyish and plump. Without the vicious scar that ran across one cheek, his face would have been forgettable.

Bill Burton was one of the few Service people that Apple knew well, or fairly well, having been on missions with him more than once. While the scar prevented Burton from being an agent in the field, he operated in several categories, from driver to back-up man.

His appearance here could be a coincidence, Apple thought. He felt sure of it when now he saw Bill Burton stop to speak to a patron. Apple arranged his features in a blank stare in case the agent looked this way.

He didn't. He moved on to talk briefly to another man, and then another. In each case, the patron shook his head. Bill Burton circled a table, glanced at Apple and came across.

Stooping, he said, "Excuse me, but are you the owner of that ex-taxi outside?"

Apple dropped his blank expression. "Why, yes," he said, overdoing it. "I certainly am."

"Well, I'm sorry but it's got my car blocked in. I wonder if you'd be kind enough to . . . ?"

"I most absolutely would."

With an excuse-me to Sylvia, Apple got up and followed the scar-faced agent, who had moved away. He wondered if it was his imagination or was the floor really uneven. Some of these new buildings, he knew, were just thrown together.

Apple moved up close behind the agent. He asked, "What is it, Bill?"

Over his shoulder Bill Burton said in a quiet tone, "An order. Depending on a question, which is: any progress with the lady?"

"Well, not exactly."

"Too bad, old son."

"What d'you mean?"

Bill Burton passed through the lounge exit, crossed the lobby and went out onto the entrance porch. Stopping, turning to face Apple, he said in clear tones that the other car had gone now, there was no need to move the ex-taxi-cab. In an undertone he added, "Angus Watkin is pulling you out. As of immediately. Make any excuse you like to the lady, and fade. Sorry about that. See you, old son."

Dazed, Apple wandered back across the hotel lobby. He felt as though he had been slapped in the face by a sweet old lady whom he had sincerely been trying to assist. He couldn't believe what he had heard.

But that the mission had ended for him was true, he knew. Unless he could think up something to hurry along the process of getting close to Sylvia; something that not only would keep him in, but also keep out another operative who could well try a tough approach.

Apple stood in the doorway to the cocktail lounge. Sylvia was gazing around placidly. She looked so attractive that Apple felt a deep twinge of regret. Being out of the caper meant that he could never see her again. It would be career suicide to try. The only possible hope was that she might turn out to be straight.

And, Apple thought, it would at least be some consolation if she proved to be the reverse, a hard-line Sickle. Then he wouldn't feel so bad about the loss.

Standing on in the doorway, swaying slightly, Apple imagined that he was trying to conjure up an excuse, one that would reasonably explain his sudden departure now and total absence in the future.

He found himself walking forward. Since he had no excuse yet, he wondered what he was doing.

Prominent among the tables stood the cocktail-lounge manager. Typically, he looked like an elder statesman: hair white at the temples, camel-angle head, morning suit with carnation buttonhole. In surveying patrons and staff, his eyes had a flasher's crafty slide and dart.

Apple stopped in front of the manager with a military crispness. He held his arms at a belligerent crook, elbows out. He glared like a preacher at coughers.

The manager looked up imperiously, swung high on his toes and asked a nasal, "May I be of service?"

Apple's answer came out loud enough to be heard in the street. He snapped, "It's outrageous!"

At once, silence clicked into being at the closer tables. It rippled outward to others as patrons stopped asking what was happening and pinpointed the noise's source. Silence was total for Apple's next loud outburst: "How dare you?"

The manager had changed his expression slowly from hauteur to disbelief. This kind of thing simply didn't happen in his domain, he seemed to be implying, therefore the offender ought to do a vanishing act.

Although he still didn't know what he was doing, Apple did own one important piece of information: he was not embarrassed. Which was mildly amazing. It could only mean that he was drunk.

But did he look it? He should. He didn't want Sylvia to think he was the kind of idiot who would pull a stroke like this when sober.

Waving his arms elaborately, Apple bellowed, "It's a damn disgrace!"

The manager, his face now empty with shock, backed away hastily. Apple followed, still waving like a traffic cop in quick time. He almost threw himself off balance. Dropping his arms, he made do with a loud hiccough as he stumped after the manager, who gasped, "What's wrong, sir? What is it?"

Low as it was, the gasp travelled well across the silence, which had an essence of delight. Apple didn't dare to look around to see how Sylvia was taking all this.

From a table he grabbed up a glass. He emptied it in two large gulps, gagged on the raw whisky and nearly brought it up again. With a groan he tossed the glass over his shoulder. The room swam.

Wading forward, Apple spluttered, "You're not going to get away with this."

"Please, please," the manager said, wafting his hands

downwards as though he were patting infant heads. "I don't know what's wrong."

"Don't play games with me!"

"If you would please calm yourself, sir."

"I am the calmest man in this place!" Apple shouted as he lurched ahead.

The manager took a new direction in his reversing. He came to a sudden stop and sat down. He sat on a woman's lap. She, thin and plain, began to blush.

Clicking out of his role, which he didn't understand anyway, Apple stepped across. He jerked the cringing elder statesman to his feet, grinned at the woman sympathetically and reassuringly, gave her arm a good squeeze and then turned to the manager to apologise.

He saw two waiters. Young and burly, they were approaching with faces of enjoyable determination. One was even miming the rolling up of sleeves.

"Are you in on this too?" Apple shouted. "Are you also on the side of the capitalists?"

Ah, he thought shrewdly, so *that's* what I'm doing. Yes, not a bad idea.

Looking uncertain, the waiters came to a halt. Apple swung around and went after the manager, who was continuing his untidy retreat. His carnation was missing.

Apple ranted, "You capitalist slave-drivers are all alike. No thought for the man in the street. No respect for freedom. No notion of equality."

The manager shook his head in denial, there were hisses from around the lounge, two people clapped and a woman called out a shrill "Rubbish!"

At a bellow, Apple reeled off all the slogans he could remember relating to anticapitalism. Next he did the same with pro-Communist slogans. In a misty, swirly sort of way, he was having a fine time.

Apple was about to go into a description of what would happen to the cocktail-lounge manager, come the revolution, when he felt his arm grabbed, from behind.

He had time to glimpse a policeman's uniform before he was jolted into a stoop by pain. His wrist had been put between his shoulder-blades in the come-along hold.

"Walk straight on, mate," the constable said, taking his prisoner forward. "The party's over."

"You don't understand, Officer."

"Just keep on walking. You ought to be ashamed of yourself. Man your height."

Apple knew several ways to break the hold, from the mere damaging to the lethal. Trouble was, he couldn't recall any of them right now.

He said, "Officer, I'm a man of peace."

"Sure you are," the policeman said. "All peaceable men have bandages on their fists."

To a background of lively talk, plus one or two subdued cheers, Apple and his captor threaded through tables towards the exit. Apple was still in a stoop, but that kept his shoulder from hurting. A bigger problem was that the constable repeatedly stepped on his heels.

This happened again now as a female voice shouted "Stop!" Apple obeyed. The policeman had to. At their side appeared Sylvia.

She asked coolly, "Just what, Officer, do you think you're doing with my friend?"

"Running him in, miss," the constable said.

"On what charge, pray?"

"The usual thing. Drunk and disorderly. We average three a week from this place, you know. The station's close by, see. Handy."

Sylvia said, "I suggest you let him go."

"Sorry," the policeman said. He pushed Apple on.

They went through into the lobby, where they came to another abrupt halt, this time because of the captor. He braked when Sylvia reappeared and pulled on his arm.

He said, "Now listen, you."

In grim deliberation, Sylvia drew back her right leg. The kick she released with force landed on the policeman's shin, evidently, for he let go of his hold in time with a hoarse yell.

Onlookers gasped, Apple staggered away into a reversing turn, the constable hopped on one leg with his face contorted, and Sylvia shouted, "Run, Russ!" She set off at speed across the lobby.

Following in a reckless weave, Apple reflected sadly that this, her response to his pro-Communist performance, surely meant that the mystery of Sylvia was solved: she had to be KGB.

A doorman tried to stop them, holding his arms out like a welcoming lover. Sylvia slipped under one, Apple crashed past the other. They went outside and ran along beside the kerb-parked cars.

Ethel, distinctive in the brilliant street lamps, was some fifty yards away. Apple, in the rear, shouted that he hoped Sylvia could drive.

She called back, "Yes, I can."

And what Sickle couldn't? Apple thought.

He skewed a look behind as he ran. By the hotel entrance, the doorman and a handful of people were standing. There was no sign of the injured policeman.

In turning his head back, Apple became dizzy and lost his equilibrium. He went careening sideways. Only the presence of a parked car prevented him from falling. He sagged there.

Sylvia came running back. Grasping his undamaged

hand, she pulled Apple into movement and began towing him at a trot along the street. Before they reached Ethel, she took him through cars to the roadway.

So that those watching outside the hotel wouldn't see which car they got into, Apple thought in glum appreciation. Neat. The act of a trained agent.

"Give me the keys," Sylvia said urgently when they stopped beside the ex-taxi.

Apple fumbled on the outsides of pockets. "Now where did I put those bloody things?"

"Come *on*, Russ. Quick."

But his touch met no familiar lump. He said, "Maybe I left 'em in the ignition."

He had, Sylvia reported on looking inside. She opened both doors. "Let's go."

Seconds later, she was shooting Ethel away from the kerb. Her gear-shifting and general control were skilled enough to be noticeable, even without taking into consideration the fact that she had never driven this car before.

Apple sprawled on the seat. He sighed at not being able to enjoy the excitement of the get-away because of his drabness over Sylvia's true occupation.

Or so the clues allege, Apple amended, offering a token resistance in the name of fairness if not feeling.

Ethel sped bowlingly along the quiet, evening street. After swinging her with squealy tyres around a corner, Sylvia said, "We made it."

"You're fabulous."

"How you doing, Russ?"

"I rather think I'm going to be sick," Apple said hollowly. He didn't know if this was true or not, but it seemed the right thing to say.

"Hold on."

"I will. Don't worry, I will." The thought of soiling

Ethel's immaculate interior had made him feel nauseous. "Shanks for everything, by the way. I mean thanksh."

"My pleasure," Sylvia said. She reduced to a normal speed. "But what started you off?"

"Ah. Yes. Tell you tomorrow." Curling up on the seat, which wasn't easy, he watched the passed and passing lights that flashed on Sylvia's hair.

"Wake up."

"I'm awake," Apple said, opening his eyes. He saw that Ethel had stopped and that Sylvia was looking in at him through the open door. "More or less."

"Up you get, Russ."

They were in Earl's Court, Apple realised as he alighted and slewed across to the house with the portico. Inside, he was pushed up two flights of stairs and into a living-room. It was neat without being a threat.

Slooping himself into an armchair, Apple mumbled, "Black coffee."

Sylvia headed into a kitchen. "Nonsense. Coffee only makes a dozy drunk into a wide-awake one." She reappeared promptly with a jug and a glass. "Water. Drink at least three glassfuls."

Glad that his performance of being drunk was going over so well, Apple added a hiccough. It made him spill the water that had just been handed to him. He grinned at that as he drank, which made the first few mouthfuls dribbly. But he finished the glass, and then two more.

"There you are," Sylvia said. "That'll calm your stomach now, and weaken your hangover tomorrow. Next thing you need is a shower. That way."

In a short passage Apple found two open doorways, one to a bedroom and one to a bathroom. In the latter he began to strip—after glancing furtively at a washing-line only to see that the small white items hanging there were gloves.

The bathroom's lighting was poor, Apple sagely acknowledged. That was why there were problems with his tie, why buttons continually slipped out of his fingers, and why he had to lie on the floor to take his shoes and socks off.

In the shower, Apple got his head under the nozzle by bending severely at the knees. Set at tepid, he let the water drum down on him at full force.

Presently, he found that the poor lighting wasn't bothering his mind so much. He was able to think with clarity, and the first thought that came to him was that he had just deliberately, blatantly disobeyed a direct order from Angus Watkin.

But his career life might be spared, Apple mused, as he would be passing on to Watkin the information that Sylvia was a Sickle. Probably. And he might even be forgiven in full if now she trusted him enough to take him into her confidence. So he needed to act forcefully.

Apple switched the shower off and got out of the stall. Noting that his bandage was sodden, he took it off and threw it in a waste-basket—though not without a twinge of regret: he had liked bearing the evidence of a wound received in the line of duty.

While drying himself, slowly because of that poor lighting, Apple sought for an answer to Sylvia's question of what had started him off in the cocktail lounge.

He was settling on the least absurd of several ideas, and thinking highly of his common sense, when there sounded a knock on the closed door followed by, "Would you like some tea and toast, Russ?"

"Yes, please," Apple said, to answer turning towards the door but covering himself with the towel.

"You need to eat something," Sylvia said. "It'll be ready in five minutes."

"Great." That he refrained from asking if she happened to have some lemon marmalade he considered decent of him, good guestmanship.

Dry, Apple wrapped the towel around his midriff and eased open the door. He stepped out cautiously. Noises and humming were coming from the kitchen.

Act forcefully, Apple reminded himself as he stepped straight across the passage and into the other room. With his guestmanship in mind, he went to the side of the double bed which had none of the bedside flotsam that informed of regular usage.

Towel off, Apple got under the covers. He lay on his back and smiled cagily at the ceiling. He had no trouble in ignoring the fact that his feet were sticking out at the bottom.

In a moment, Sylvia appeared in the doorway. "Oh," she said. "There you are."

Apple said, "Yes."

"You've taken the bandage off. How's your hand?"

"It's a little bit swollen. I can use it." He coughed delicately.

Sylvia came forward. "Let me see, Russ."

When she took his hand, Apple reversed the movement and drew her down. They embraced. They kissed. It happened easily and smoothly.

At first they pecked tenderly at each other's lips as though they were goodies not to be gorged. Next, the kisses became more suggestive, imitative.

Sylvia eased her mouth free. Softly she said, "Let me up. I'll get undressed."

Apple, hoarsely: "Good."

"But close your eyes, Russ. I'm shy."

Apple closed his eyes.

Apple fell asleep.

His feet woke him up. They were cold. On opening his eyes to see what he was doing while rubbing his feet together to create warmth, he found that he was embracing a woman.

After an interval of nothingness, Apple remembered the where and how and who of the situation. He smiled. He forgot about his feet.

Sylvia mumbled, "You awake?"

"Yes," Apple said. "Good morning."

"Good morning. How do you feel?" She still lay with her head on his chest.

"Fine. No headache."

Sylvia pushed herself up, thus revealing that she was naked—apart from her gloves. She looked at Apple and told him that water worked wonders.

Unaware that his feet were rubbing themselves together like anticipating hands, Apple said in a meaningful voice, "As I was saying last night . . ."

She came back into his arms and they kissed. The kiss lasted a long time. Apple counted Sylvia's vertebrae. His feet were still and taut.

When the kiss paused, Sylvia murmured erotically, "Take my gloves off."

Later, much later, when Apple was sitting up in bed, waiting for coffee and cold toast, he reflected that although his romantic hopes in respect of Sylvia were doomed, because of her nationality and job, he *had* made love to a beautiful espionage agent. He would have to make hay of the here and now, not give himself up to wistful thinking.

Sylvia came in with a tray. She wore a see-through

flimsy that reached her thighs, and gloves whose cuffs were turned wantonly down. Slipping into bed, she set the tray between herself and Apple, who told her she was one in a hundred million.

"You're not exactly run-of-the-mill yourself, Russ."

"Well, I certainly wasn't last night."

Sylvia handed him a mug of coffee. "What started you off on your tantrum?"

"A remark made by that manager character," Apple said. "I overheard it as I was walking out with the man who wanted to get his car unblocked. He heard it as well, and laughed, which added fuel to flame."

"The remark was?"

"Something along the lines of the Reds being idiots."

"Reds meaning Communists, I suppose."

Apple helped himself to a piece of toast. "Right. And my parents were hard-liners. My old man fought in the Spanish Civil War, against fascist Franco. So you see, I was brought up with communism."

"Mmm," Sylvia commented indifferently, chewing.

Apple wondered if he had sounded unconvincing; if, in fact, his whole performance from cocktail lounge to here was too obvious to be believable. He sighed.

"I'll tell you a secret," he said.

"Lovely."

"I've been lying to you."

Sylvia glanced at him. "Is that right?"

"I told you that my middle name was Russell. It isn't. I was christened Appleton Russia."

"Hey, that's cute."

"Silly, I think," Apple said, pulling a face. "But it does show how very strongly my parents felt about the cause. I'm not that rabid myself, although I am, certainly, a Communist sympathiser."

Sylvia, nodding, went on with her snack. Apple did the same, falling silent. He had no way of knowing if he had scored or made matters worse, and, looking down sideways at Sylvia's ripe breasts, he didn't really care.

Wiping her lips on a paper napkin, Sylvia said casually, "To me, all political systems are boring. But if I had to make a choice between democracy and communism, I'd take democracy like a shot. Sorry about that, Russ."

Apple winked. "There's one thing I refuse to do when I'm in bed with a beautiful woman, and that's talk politics."

"Is there one thing you do insist on doing?"

"Yes," Apple said firmly. "The removal of obstacles. Such as this tray."

Some time later they got up and took a shower together. Apple told himself that his ploy, which had seemed so clever last night, had failed. Therefore he could expect from Angus Watkin the rocket of his life or a firing squad. He still didn't care. He hummed while soaping Sylvia's back.

"You sound happy, Russ."

"I am. Aren't you?"

Sylvia turned to him suddenly. "Listen," she said. "It's my turn to tell secrets."

Apple rubbed a hand wetly over his face in case it was showing the dither of excitement he felt. "Your name's really George?"

"Seriously. The reason I wear gloves most of the time. It's nothing to do with sensitivity."

"It's not?"

Looking up at him eye to eye, Sylvia said, "It's because of allergies. I'm allergic to almost everything. My fingers come out in ugly red blotches."

Returning her gaze steadily, Apple gave slow nods.

They were for himself. He was agreeing with his instinctive impression that Sylvia had spoken the entire truth.

She added, "So there's no real connection with picking pockets."

"I see."

"Which leads us to secret number two." She stepped out of the stall and picked up a towel. "I, Russ for Russia, am not a pickpocket."

Apple revived his dying act of nodding, which he did for the same reason as before. He also donned an expression of bewilderment.

"I don't understand," he said. He switched off the water and came out, catching the towel that was tossed to him by Sylvia, who said, "Though I don't think I do too badly at it for a novice. A friend gave me a cram course. She's dipping her way through college."

Apple said, "I'm amazed." He meant it. He almost added that he was relieved, but he wasn't quite there yet. He was still absorbing the fact that he might have been very wrong about Sylvia.

Apple shook his head, knowing he would get a negative, as he asked, "And all that was so you could do research into pickpocketing?"

Sylvia did a hula against the towel she was holding taut behind her hips. "No, Russ, it wasn't."

"Then I'm still in the dark."

"That story, I'm afraid, was another lie. Though not a harmful one. I had to say something to explain my interest in other pickpockets, didn't I?"

"Well, I suppose so."

With the towel over her hand, Sylvia unpinned a pair of gloves from the line. She put them on, which increased the allure of her nakedness.

Turning to leave the room, she said, "I'll make us some fresh coffee. And explain."

Apple quickly finished drying himself, quickly dressed. He declined to speculate on what was coming next from this mysterious girl. Leaving his hair uncombed, rakish, he went to the kitchen.

Sylvia looked around from the stove. "Take a pew, Russ." She was wearing a sweater and jeans, but Apple told himself it didn't matter, it didn't matter in the least.

He squeezed into a cramped breakfast nook, saying, "You've got me guessing, Sylvia."

She told him over her shoulder, voice quiet, "I'm here in London to do a job, Russ."

"You're working for somebody?"

"You could put it that way. But I'm not getting paid. Let's say it's something I *have* to do."

"Well now," Apple said. "I don't know if I care for the sound of that."

In two steps Sylvia came to the table with coffee. She sat and slid one mug across to Apple. They lit cigarettes and looked at each other through the smoke.

Sylvia said, "I'm playing detective. I'm trying to find a particular man. Or it might be a woman. He or she is a pickpocket."

"Missing person?"

"No. I don't know anything about this dip. I have no information on age, sex, description, type. I only know that he—let's assume it's a man—picked the pocket of a particular someone recently. In Piccadilly Station. I have to find that dip and try to get the lifted item back."

"Now it's sounding impossible."

"No, just difficult," Sylvia said. "Because I do have the time of the dip."

"Well, that might be a bit of help."

"It happened last Thursday at three-thirty in the afternoon."

Again hoping that he wasn't showing his dither of excitement, Apple looked down into his coffee. Thursday at half past three was when Narkov, the cultural attaché from the Soviet Embassy, was found dead. On a platform of Piccadilly Station.

Sylvia said, "So if I could meet a dip who was working there then, he's got to be the one. Or he can tell me of others who were there. And he would of course cooperate, so long as he believes that I'm a dip myself."

"Yes, I can understand the need for all the camouflage," Apple said. "But who is the someone you're doing this for? Is he male?"

"Yes."

"Lover? Husband?"

Sylvia shook her head emphatically. "Nothing of that nature. Otherwise you wouldn't be here."

Apple liked that. But he warned himself that he was asking too many questions. It wouldn't do for this to seem like an interrogation.

Apple asked, "So who is this man?"

Sylvia gave her head another firm shake. "Sorry, Russ. I'm not free to tell you anything about him. That's final."

"Okay, okay," Apple said soothingly. "Let's not give him another thought."

"Thanks, Russ."

"But the item that got lifted. The one you have to find. What was it?"

"I don't know."

"What?"

"I don't know. But it's sure to be something distinctive, memorable. And, of course, small enough to be slipped easily in and out of a pocket."

Trying not to sound incredulous, Apple asked, "You really don't know what the item is?"

Easing forward, Sylvia put a glove on his arm and looked at him searchingly. "I do not. Absurd though it sounds, I have no idea what I'm looking for. Believe me."

Apple, nodding, did. He again had the instinctive impression that he was hearing the truth.

"Well, well, well," he said, his spirits up. "This is a pretty strange situation."

"And don't I know it."

Lifting their mugs, they sipped. Apple was the busiest sipper. It gave him something to do with his continuing dither. He also tapped one foot.

After a moment Sylvia said, "I'd be very grateful if you could help me."

Apple put his mug down. "I will. Gladly. If I can think up a way to go about it."

"Those dips I met. They know me now. Maybe if I went back to see them."

"No," Apple said. "There has to be a short-cut. I'll have to give the matter some thought. I'm sure to come up with something."

"Russ for Russia," Sylvia said, smiling richly, "you are an absolute gem."

Apple looked at his watch. "One without a job, if I don't check in at work."

On emerging from the house, his step sprightly, Apple turned left in the direction of a main road, where he recalled seeing a telephone box. He had to call in soonest.

Apple's step lost some of its spring when he noticed, ahead, a man pushing himself up from a lean on a car. His eyes were on Apple, who thought, if that character isn't an agent of some kind, I'm a short-arse.

He veered aside, intending to cross the street. At once he saw another man with the bland stamp of an espionage operative. This one, about to come over the road, was also looking his way.

Apple swung around. He walked briskly. That he didn't glance behind was because (a) he knew that the men would be coming, and (b) his eyes were occupied busily with scanning the way ahead.

He wasn't surprised to see yet another agent type. The man was getting out of a car, from its rear. When upright, he stood holding the door open.

Before Apple could start planning moves, a fourth man had joined the scene. He got out of the driver's seat of the same car as number three. He was Bill Burton.

His tension running down, Apple changed to a jaunty walk. He wanted to make it clear that he was not the renegade that this pick-up party seemed to be stating.

Apple reached the car. "Good morning, gents," he said. "I was just on my way to call in."

His face as expressive as a clock's, Bill Burton said, "Let's go." He began to get back behind the steering-wheel. The other man said boredly, "In you get."

Apple gave a bright smile. "Why, thank you. A lift would be quite handy."

One minute later they were moving off, Apple and number three in the back. The other pair of agents had done a fade.

Apple didn't try to catch Bill Burton's eye in the rear-view mirror. He knew that even though the scar-faced agent might have sympathy to offer, or could advise on how to play the next scene, neither would be forthcoming —in any form of communication. The third man's presence ruled that out.

In any case, as Apple further knew, Bill Burton would

have to be cautious. If the assumed renegade was, in fact, just that, or should he get kicked out of the Service anyway, for disobeying orders, Burton would need to cut him deader than a lead soldier, if only because of past association. Your security rating was all. It and you had to be protected on every flank in a profession where even men at the top could turn out to be traitors.

Presently, the car came into Regent Street. Parking spaces being as profuse as empty pubs, Bill Burton stopped beside the standing vehicles. In doing so, he sent behind a fast wink via the mirror.

"Thanks, Arnold," Apple said. "For the lift."

Burton grunted, "Sure."

Alighting, Apple went to the building's doorway with agent number three, who was big and heavy.

An obvious one-man mob, Apple mused. The type who could reduce you to pulp while watching a pretty girl go by, and at the same time quoting the Marquis of Queensberry rules to show he had a sense of humour.

They went inside and up the stairs. There was silence between them except for one exchange. The man said, "His name isn't Arnold." Apple said, "All spies look alike to me."

Number three opened the door of Trident Imports, jerked his head, and closed himself out when Apple had passed inside.

From the inner room strolled Angus Watkin. If he was angry, it didn't show, although there could have been a message in the way he stayed on the threshold, just as Apple was staying by the outer door.

They spoke across the room to each other. Apple said good morning and what a nice day it was; his Control said that a storm might be brewing.

Pleasantries thus dispensed with, Apple went quickly

on the attack, the while holding his head at an angle of smug confidence.

He said he knew that Mr. Watkin would have understood when his operative failed to step out of the mission as ordered, realising at once that said operative must be on to something. Success, in fact.

Apple used the phrase "my success" frequently as he went on to detail last night's events, including his act of being inebriated, one kicked policeman, a smooth getaway, his tactical advance of finally getting into Sylvia's apartment, his charge toward victory by wheedling his way into her bed.

Angus Watkin asked, "Did you have sexual congress with the young lady, Porter?"

"I did," Apple said, dropping his voice. Being a kiss-and-teller was a highly essential part of his job, but he didn't like it, particularly now, when the woman involved was Sylvia.

"And she talked afterwards? Is that the victory, the success you've mentioned eleven times?"

"Yes, sir. She confessed that she'd been lying before, and told me the truth of why she was here."

Angus Watkin nearly raised an eyebrow. "You mean, surely, that she changed her story. You couldn't possibly know whether or not it was the truth."

"Well no, I suppose not," Apple mumbled. With more clarity he added, "I believe her all the same."

"Have we, one wonders, conceived a romantic passion for this young lady?"

Coldly: "Certainly not, sir."

"I see," Watkin said. "Oh well."

"Truly, sir."

"Pray continue with what it is that you believe."

Apple related Sylvia's story, ending on, "The pocket

in question was picked at around three-thirty last Thursday, at Piccadilly."

Angus Watkin gave one long, slow nod. "Quite, Porter. We must assume, therefore, that the victim of pickpocketry was the late Narkov."

"It appears so, sir, yes."

"Excellent."

"But I feel sure that Sylvia isn't KGB. It's true that she refused to go into details, name names, but there could be many reasons for that."

"Yes?"

"Yes," Apple said. "Maybe she's under pressure by the opposition, without knowing what they are. Maybe she's doing this for someone who *is* an agent. Maybe there's a family member behind the Iron Curtain, the hostage routine. Yes indeed, many reasons."

"Time will tell, Porter. But that, in any case, is of no consequence."

"It isn't?"

Watkin shook his head. "What the girl is doesn't matter, now that we know the motive for her presence."

Back to smugness, Apple said, "I'm glad I was able to pull it off, sir. We might never have found out if I hadn't ignored that order."

"But you were meant to ignore it, Porter," Angus Watkin said lazily.

Apple blinked. "I was what?"

"I gave the order with the hopes of shocking you into a new line of action."

"Oh."

"The ploy worked, I'm pleased to say," Angus Watkin said. He turned to the door behind him. "Come along, Porter. We're going to the movies."

They passed through one room where a man, doing a newspaper's crossword puzzle, sat beside a silent radio receiver. In the next room another man was bending over a film projector. It and a spinney of bentwood chairs were the only furnishings. Lights were on, the window was covered.

"I'd like number eight, please," Angus Watkin said. "The shorter version."

"Yes, sir," the projectionist said.

Watkin, copied by Apple, sat on a chair. They were facing a blank white wall. With a click the room's light was reduced to half-strength. The machine began to hum and a square yard of flickery brightness appeared on the whitewash.

"This film," Angus Watkin said, "was taken on the afternoon of Narkov's death."

It was a street scene. With ease, Apple recognised London's Chinatown, that cramped area between Leicester Square and Shaftesbury Avenue. The large, colourful signs that climbed the buildings were all in Chinese script. Most of the pedestrians had Oriental features.

Watkin said, "Our man is the one in the trilby."

The camera being at double human height (in a window, Apple judged), the man from the Soviet Embassy could be seen clearly in the crowd. Of late middle-age, he was tall and heavily built. He wore his hat pulled uncompromisingly down to his ears. His overcoat had the high shoulders of Iron Curtain tailoring.

Apple found it strange to be watching a man who was about to die. He tried not to look too closely at the heavy, seamed face and the deep-set eyes.

Narkov entered one of the Chinese business establishments. Immediately, the film jumped, and the Russian was coming out to the street.

"Restaurant," Angus Watkin said. "The time lapse was forty-eight minutes."

The film jumped to a different street scene. From a scruffy pavement vendor, Narkov was buying a newspaper. He walked on reading, which he continued to do for five minutes, tracked by the camera (under cover on a hand-barrow, Apple guessed). After Narkov had tossed his paper into a trash-can on a lamp-post, the scene changed again.

Now it was the exterior of an Italian ice-cream parlour. The Russian went inside and came out again, with a split between which Angus Watkin reported as representing seven minutes.

The next location was near a busy corner. Narkov stood with his back to the wall while a shoeshine man tended to his shoes. Throughout the operation, which the camera recorded, there seemed to be no conversation between the man and his customer.

Another jump in the film, and the cultural attaché was lowering himself onto a bench in Leicester Square. It then looked, comically, as if the film were being reversed, but it was only Narkov rising from his bench after another cut.

"He stayed there for thirty-three minutes," Angus Watkin said. "He was approached by nobody. His interest, apparently, was given only to the prettier of the women who passed by."

Next, the man from the embassy went into a Danish pastry shop. It had an elegant façade. The cut before Narkov's reappearance, Apple heard from his chief, represented four and a quarter minutes.

A new scene was flashed on the wall. The camera stayed with Narkov during his purchase of cigarettes from a kiosk and his stopping of a passer-by to get a light and his throwing away of the cigarette after three puffs.

Apple recognised the last establishment to be visited by the Russian. It was a kosher snack bar in Soho. Narkov was in there only two minutes.

The film ended.

As the lights came on, Angus Watkin said over his shoulder, "Thank you. That's all." When the door had closed behind the projectionist, he turned to Apple with: "The rest of it we were unable to film. However, I can give it to you briefly. Our late friend went to Piccadilly Station, where he bought a ticket for Queensway and descended to the platform. A train came in. Nine tenths of the people there got on it. Narkov stayed. When the train had left, he dropped to the ground. The remainder you already know."

Apple nodded. "But not the beforehand, sir."

"It was more or less a muchness with what you've seen, Porter. On his previous free Thursday afternoons, Narkov went through similar motions, but the only place he ever called at more than once was that shoeshine pitch."

"It checked out innocent, obviously."

"It and all the other stops," Angus Watkin said. "Also innocent were the thrown-away newspaper, the discarded cigarette and the packet it came from."

Feeling clever, Apple asked, "How about the man who gave Narkov a light?"

"By coincidence, one of my own people."

Back to feeling a faceless one, Apple said, "Maybe Narkov was giving out or receiving signals. Body language, blinks in Morse code, the business with that cigarette—any of the standard forms of no-contact communication."

"The full films have been studied carefully," Angus Watkin said in a voice that was duller than normal. "By experts. But thank you anyway for the suggestion."

Apple murmured, "Welcome."

"So, Porter, it seems reasonable to assume that our Narkov picked up an item of import at one of his stops that last day. Either it came from someone connected with the place itself, or from someone he met there."

"Was he not under observation by operatives when out of camera reach?"

After a Watkin sigh: "Naturally, Porter. Everywhere. And nothing untoward was seen. But that does not mean, of course, that an item did not change hands. In fact, your information makes it almost certain that it did."

Apple raised his eyebrows. "Quite, sir. I thought the info might come in handy."

"And that item," Angus Watkin said, as though he had heard nothing, "was stolen from Narkov by a common pickpocket. Or so the Russians believe."

"It could've been an agent who did the dip, sir. One from another organization."

"That, Porter, is entirely possible. But the continuing presence of other foreign operatives makes it look as though the Russians could be right. They often are, actually."

If his Control did have a saving grace as a human being, Apple mused, it was that he didn't put down or scorn an enemy. He had less liking for the UK's Naval Intelligence than he had for the KGB.

"Therefore," Angus Watkin said, "I must now do what the Russians are trying to do—find the pertinent pickpocket. And find him first."

Apple, crisply: "Yes, sir."

"Which task, Porter, is in *my* hands."

Apple, limply: "Oh."

"Your job is now finished in that respect. What I want you to do from here on is occupy yourself with the young lady. You have burned no bridges, I trust."

"No, sir. We're on the closest of terms. She gave me her telephone number."

"I could have given it to you days ago, Porter. You ought to have asked."

And you, Apple thought, ought to have offered it to me. But then you would've missed that warming I-knew-all-along bit of business, minor though it was.

"My people will find the pickpocket, if he's findable," Angus Watkin said. "You just stick close to the young lady. Keep her out of the way, and keep her out of other hands." He began to get up. "That's all, Porter. Good morning."

FIVE

Apple walked home. In the entrance hall at Harlequin Mansions he checked on the centre table to see if he had mail. He hadn't, but the thought was a reminder.

Upstairs, he typed a letter of apology to the cocktail lounge's manager and staff, signing it with one of the names he had always fancied for himself, Dirk Steel. With it in the envelope he folded a five-pound note to cover damages.

That sum he put on his expense sheet, along with last night's drinks. After some spiteful thought, he added the charge of an imaginary taxi-cab ride from Regent Street to Bloomsbury, since Angus Watkin had caused him to leave Ethel in Earl's Court.

Lighting a cigarette, Apple began to pace. He returned inevitably to what had been in his mind ever since leaving the makeshift cinema. The mystery pickpocket.

Apple wanted to be the one to identify him, that was the subject matter. He wanted to find the dip, get back the coveted item, and casually hand it over to a stunned Angus Watkin.

Or, Apple wondered, did he? Didn't he maybe want to give the item to Sylvia, so that her problem would be solved?

He thought about it.

Pacing, Apple shook his head. He realised that, on the far outside chance of Sylvia being KGB, it would be wrong to hand over the item to her, even though yes, that was what his emotions wanted him to do.

Apple threw his cigarette butt into the fireplace as he made a turn there. Absently forgetting that Monico wasn't present to play audience, which forgetfulness prevented him from becoming embarrassed about talking to himself, he said, "If I did get the item, however, I could examine it thoroughly. And, if it wasn't harmful to the West, nor too outrageously helpful to the Soviets, *then* I could gift Sylvia with what she needs."

Apple nodded his agreement. Pacing faster, he said, "It wouldn't be wrong to look for the pickpocket, you know. Not terribly. I mean, let's face it, old Angus didn't *order* me to stay out of it. In fact, he might actually be hoping that I *will* nose in on the act, knowing that I do have these flashes of brilliance."

Apple left that with a self-conscious cough, which he pretended not to notice. He also ignored the pretence.

"Poetic justice," he said. "That's what it'd be if I found the item. One in the eye for the odious Watkin. Furthermore I could be put on the first step of the flight that leads to Upstairs. Further furthermore I'd be a hero to Sylvia. Her hero for ever."

Smiling, Apple stopped by a window and looked out. He saw not the street below but a scene of Sylvia displaying awe and gratitude eternal. It was a lengthy reverie.

When Apple sighed out of it, he thought of the reverse result: what could happen to Sylvia if the Brits or other agents got hold of the item.

Apple made up his mind. He was going to try to locate the unknown pickpocket. Which left him with only one question. How was he going to go about it?

With thudding strides, Apple went to his kitchen. He plugged in the toaster, put the kettle on to boil, began slicing bread. There was no better brain food he knew of than tea served with toast that bore lemon-flavoured marmalade, which also, conveniently, happened to be his favourite snack.

Soon Apple was sitting at the table. He sipped tea and crunched toast while seeking ideas.

The first that came to him was bribery. If he could find the heavy who had warned him off at the station (which should be fairly easy), he could offer a royal sum to be helped with the search. Creating a cover story would be child's play. But would the heavy cooperate?

The telephone rang.

Tutting at the interruption, Apple headed for his living-room. He would have ignored the shrill summons except for the fact that not answering telephones always made him feel like a cynic.

The caller was Harlequin Mansions' landlord. He, ever on the trail of illicit pets, wanted to know if Apple had heard miaows in the night. Apple disconnected after assuring the landlord that he had heard nothing more unusual than a few yaps and yelps.

Enjoying his conviction that he was developing into quite a wit, Apple returned to his snack. Hardly had he started on the first lovely mouthful, smiling, before he discovered a possible solution.

Which was Alf. A friend of Apple's, Alf was the landlord of a pub. It was said of Alf, most frequently by Alf himself, that he knew every criminal in London.

Apple laughed with success, spreading gooey crumbs. He gave full marks to his favourite food for helping him to come up with the idea of landlord Alf. Calming, he ate on with doubled appreciation.

Stickiness licked off his fingers, Apple went to the telephone. He dialled Sylvia and told her he had remembered an underworld connection they could try, one who knew more dips than a chocolate factory.

"Wonderful," Sylvia said. "And listen, since I have the car keys, why don't I drive over there and pick you up?"

"Better still," Apple said, "you could meet me in Piccadilly Circus." He thought it wouldn't hurt to first try to see the heavy in the station below, as a hope to fall back on in case Alf was unable to help.

"What time, Russ?"

"Well, this friend of mine, he's the guv'nor of a boozer. He'll have the time to talk to us after he closes this afternoon. So let's say three o'clock."

"Right," Sylvia said. "And thanks, Russ. You're sensational. In more ways than one."

Almost blushing, Apple mumbled a goodbye and rang off. His next call was to Alf. He told him to expect visitors, that his name was Russ and that he was a pickpocket—an explanation to be given some other time. Alf sounded intrigued. After disconnecting, Apple headed for his bedroom to have a nap.

At two o'clock sharp, following a shave plus a change into wind-cheater and jeans, Apple went downstairs and out to the street. He walked at a steady pace, one that would get him to the Circus in reasonable time. On the first corner he paused to post his letter to the cocktail lounge.

When near the British Museum, Apple suddenly turned. He set off back, quickening his pace until he was striding. Next he began to jog. Over the final hundred yards, he ran. He didn't stop running until he was at the door of his flat.

Inside, Apple went straight to his writing desk and grabbed up a pen and bent over his expense sheet and quickly scratched out the phony cab-ride fare.

Apple went down the steps into Piccadilly Station. As he moved along with the crowd, he sagged. He was only slightly taller than tall by the time he came into the circular concourse.

Moving to the wall when he had penetrated sufficiently, Apple stopped. His search for the heavy was short-lived. It went from his mind as, in gazing around, he began to pick out men who could be espionage operatives. They all had the same physical stamp and were busy doing nothing. Apple had never seen so many spooks all at one time in his life.

He sank lower, started to reverse, eased his way to the steps and went up towards daylight. The opposition, he realised, had become fierce. If Apple wasn't able to come up with something, the mystery pickpocket would be as easy to find as a pimp with a heart of gold.

On the Circus, Apple stood with other tourists and idlers by the kerbside handrail. Traffic, mostly double-decker buses, flowed past in a steady but sluggish procession.

Several times as Apple waited, he got the sensation that he was being watched. He didn't turn around to check; it would have served no purpose. In any case, he expected that these looks were merely being directed at an unusually tall person.

Ethel came into view.

"Christ, look at that bloody thing," an idler snorted, which helped dispel the twinge of jealousy that came to Apple on account of someone else being in the driver's seat. It was a further help that the driver was Sylvia.

Apple climbed over the handrail. Stepping into the road, he raised an arm and shouted, "Taxi!" Sylvia slowed enough for him to open the back door and get in. He sprawled on the seat, smiling at his boldness.

Sylvia asked, "Where to, sir?"

"The Bellringer Arms, cabby. It's in Southwark. But since you're new on the job, I'll direct you."

They kept the joke going until they were on Trafalgar Square, when Apple, looking through the window for the third time, saw that the car was still behind. It was medium-size, dull grey, and had two men in the front.

"What's so interesting back there?" Sylvia asked.

Apple said, "If you'd like to make a full circle of the square, I'll tell you."

While Sylvia was obliging, Apple kept a rear watch on the car. Because of his distance back from the window, plus the darkness of the glass (to provide privacy, as stipulated by the regulations on taxi-cabs) he had no fret about being seen by the possible tailers.

Who were still there, three vehicles back, when Sylvia had completed the extensive circuit. Apple told her the truth: that it was feasible that they were being followed, and just as feasible that he was mistaken.

He lied the rest of it: "If we are, it can only be those gangsters who got me before. Maybe they're after me again, or this is a form of warning."

"What do we do, Russ?"

"Lose 'em," Apple said. "Like they do in the movies. I always knew somehow that my passion for gangster films would come in useful one day."

"Do you want to take over?"

"No need—you're doing fine. Take that turning there, to begin with."

For thirty minutes, still heading roughly in the wanted, south-east direction, Sylvia continually turned along streets and alley-ways. Most of that time was in the name of security, for after the first several minutes Apple lost sight of the grey car.

It was almost four o'clock when they came to the public house called the Bellringer Arms. There was no moving traffic on the untidy street, which was entirely residential apart from the pub, where untidyness reached its dull apex.

Apple took Sylvia to a side door. His knock was answered by a plump man in his forties. He wore baggy corduroys and a frayed sweater. His eyes, quick and shrewd, darted all over Sylvia during greetings and introductions.

Alf led his visitors into the bar, which smelled of beer spillage, unwashed ashtrays and disinfectant. He insisted on hosting a round of drinks. Apple asked for tomato juice. Alf went behind his counter to do the serving.

Like most of Apple's friends, the pub's guv'nor was a person who had never quite made it but who lived in hope. His goal was to operate one of the exclusive hotels owned by the company that had, among its chain of hostelries, the Bellringer Arms. Apparently, Alf had never considered that his thick cockney accent and foul language would constitute a drawback.

Drinks served, cigarettes lit, Alf's wet cough waited out, Apple told about Sylvia's misfortune in having her travel papers—passport, air-ticket, traveller's cheques—lifted out of her bag by a pickpocket. She had to get them back at once and there was little the police could do to help.

"Seeing as how I'm in the same line of business," Apple said, "I can't blame the guy. But it's pretty hard on poor Sylvia." He winked the eye that was hidden from the girl at his side, the wink stating: I fancy this bird, see, and I'd tell her I'm a mass-murderer if it'd help.

That, Apple figured, was all the explanation that would be needed by Alf, himself a bird-fancier, and one who knew that many girls saw criminals in a romantic light.

"Yeh, very f—— 'ard," the landlord said, patting Sylvia's arm in sympathy. It was a long pat.

Apple: "And I thought you might be able to mark my card, you knowing more dips than I do."

Alf nodded. "Where was you dipped, you poor fing you?" he asked Sylvia.

She told him, "Piccadilly underground station."

"That's a bit of reserved terri-bleeding-tory, that is. But I might be able to 'elp. I'll give it a fink while we do in these drinks."

The doing in took time, as Alf gave most of his thinking to ways of flirting with Sylvia. Apple repeatedly cleared his throat. Sylvia asked if he was all right. Alf recommended an ocean voyage.

Finally, coming around from behind the bar, the landlord said, "I'll take a ball along the frog and 'ave a dicky with a tea."

When Alf had gone out to the street, Apple translated for Sylvia the rhyming slang. Ball-of-chalk: walk. Frog-and-toad: road. Dicky-bird: word. Tea-leaf: thief.

"He's cute," Sylvia said.

Apple said, "I like the way you drive."

Alf was back after ten minutes. He reported, "Me mate says there's only one dip left what works the West End. And that's coz she 'as a broken leg. This is 'er address." He handed over a slip of paper. "They calls 'er Fums. Fums Morgan."

"Thumbs?" Apple asked.

"Yeh—Fums."

"But what d'you mean, the only one left?"

"Well, me mate says the others've all buggered off out of town. For safety."

Apple shook his head. "I don't get you."

Alf said, "See, the 'eat's on. Every main dipping scene is just crawling wiv plain-clothes coppers."

Traffic was dense, this being the height of the evening panic. Blackfriars Bridge was one solid mass of vehicles. Ethel crawled along with Apple and Sylvia. Their pace was easily bettered by the joggers who went by the cars with amused eyebrows.

Normally, Apple wouldn't have minded the creep. He would, in fact, have enjoyed simply being out with Ethel, as well as appreciating the attention she attracted.

But now he had a feeling of urgency. It persisted even though he repeatedly assured himself that he had a head-and-shoulders start on the competition: other operatives of whatever nationality weren't going to get far in dipless London.

Sylvia, on the folding seat behind him, asked, "Do you think we're being followed?"

Which question formed part of his urgency. He said, "It's not possible to tell in this traffic."

"Perhaps when we get free of it."

"That's the problem—we won't be free of it for most of the trip. We have to go right across the middle of town. Edmonton's directly north of here."

"Well, the traffic's protection, at least," Sylvia said in a soothing tone. "If those gangsters are after you, they won't be able to get close."

No, Apple thought, but we can be followed to our lead, and from there to the next call, if there is one, and from that to wherever in the country the right dip has gone to.

"That's true," Apple said, dithering his foot impatiently on the accelerator. "In any case, they might give up out of boredom."

The creep became an ooze once they were off the bridge, but there was no improvement on that state until they had cleared Central London. Even then, however, Apple would have been able to go faster on a bicycle, and it was still not possible to tell if he had a tail. His urgency stayed high.

The house in Edmonton was detached, small and neat, with an elaborate garden where wooden birds were pulling at plastic worms. It didn't go with the occupier's name, but neither did the occupier herself.

Thumbs was a tall, slender, flash-elegant woman in her late thirties. Her cosmetics and exotic hair-do looked to have been given thorough attention five minutes ago. She wore a dress that reached her ankles; it covered most of the plaster cast that thumped as she limpingly led the visitors into a dainty parlour.

Ignoring Sylvia, Thumbs ushered Apple onto a couch and sat beside him. She fussed, smiling coquettishly. She offered him a string of refreshments, ranging from cocoa to cognac. She patted his shoulder.

Sylvia, who had taken an upright chair in the background, cleared her throat.

Politely declining all offerings, Apple got immediately to the nub. He told of the loss to a pickpocket of Sylvia's travel documents.

"Pity," Thumbs drawled in a voice like post-orgy exhaustion.

"Thanks," Sylvia said in a similar tone.

As though that were the end of the topic, Thumbs

asked Apple, "And you're in the profession yourself, did you say, darling?"

"That's right."

"How curious that I never heard of you before. How, one might phrase it, tragic."

"I play it cool."

"Charming, Russ. I'm sure you won't mind if I call you by your first name."

"But these documents," Apple said. "You know, you could even have lifted them yourself."

"Acquired," Thumbs murmured. "And it is possible, of course. Depending on the wheres and whens."

That was supplied by Sylvia. Still ignoring her, the hostess said, "Well, darling, the place is right but the time's quite, quite wrong."

Apple said, "It is?"

"It is. No professional would dream of working a station of the underground at three-thirty in the afternoon."

Apple, surprised, asked, "Why not?" Quickly he amended, "I mean, I'm mainly a queue-worker myself, and the time never makes any difference."

"I wouldn't know about that, darling. I do know that at mid-afternoon the stations have this *ghastly* lull. There's no one around except a handful of schoolchildren and penniless layabouts. Not only is it unproductive, it's also extremely dangerous. Crowds mean safety."

Apple nodded slowly, glumly. What the woman said made such sense that he wondered if the whole thing could be a big mistake, that Narkov had lost nothing to a pickpocket, that everyone, Russians included, were in error.

Thumbs said, "Don't be depressed, darling. Every cloud has a silver lining."

"I felt so sure that you'd be able to help," Apple said, blinking sadly in case that might be useful.

"I would if I could, darling. Believe me."

"*No* one would be working at that time?"

Thumbs waved a long, slim hand languidly. "No one of a real professional standing. You do get the odd semi-pro who'll go out on acquiring trips only when funds're low." She smiled abruptly. "Ah."

Apple and Sylvia unisoned, "What?"

"I might know your very man."

Apple and Sylvia unisoned, "Yes?"

"Yes," Thumbs said. "He's a magician."

Apple said, "Yes?" and Sylvia said, "What?"

"Lots of pickpockets are good at sleight of hand, obviously, and any skilled conjurer would make an excellent pickpocket."

"Right," Apple said, as if he knew all about it.

"Harry Fitch, also known as the Great Harold, takes either rabbits out of top hats or wallets out of pockets. He's just the type who'd work at the wrong time of day, if he's broke and between engagements, and I do know that he favours Piccadilly Circus."

"Where do we find him, please?" Apple asked eagerly, beginning to rise.

Thumbs drew him down again. "Let me help you, darling. I *want* to. I'll give Harry a tinkle." She reached down and aside to a telephone on the floor.

In a moment Thumbs was having a one-sided conversation about skin lotion with someone called Mavis my dear. Apple thought it would last for ever. It lasted only twenty minutes, after passing through babies, a television series, the drinking of cabbage water and good old Harry.

Thumbs said, "Bye-bye, Mavis my dear. And thanks."

Apple: "Well?"

Having dipped the cradle, Thumbs began to dial again. She said, "Harry has a gig. Out Tilbury way. I hope he gets more. It'll keep him from crowding the pitch."

Apple asked, "Does that mean the Great Harold is appearing somewhere as a conjurer?"

Thumbs nodded. "At Percy's Club."

"I know it."

"Awfully common. They say that even the mice take their own food." Her expression changed to imperious for, "Ah, good evening. I'd like to speak to the Great Harold, if you please. Thank you."

"Listen, Thumbs," Apple said quickly and quietly. "Don't tell Harry the reason. I'd like to talk to him in person. Just ask the question."

"For green eyes—" Thumbs started, then broke off to gush a greeting into the receiver. Next, she asked the question. She listened. She prompted, "Last Thursday, dear." She gave a deep nod. "Oh, you were. Great. What? Oh, well I thought I saw you then, but you know how it is . . ."

Apple was already on his feet. He hurriedly thanked Thumbs, who tried to answer him and talk to Harry at the same time, and pushed Sylvia ahead of him out of the room and out of the house.

Dusk had settled into transient place. As Apple snapped open Ethel's rear door he said, "We're on the last lap. Wasn't Thumbs a nice helpful person?"

Sylvia asked, "How far is this club?"

About twenty miles, Apple reckoned. Which wouldn't take long on the outer London highways, where traffic was heavy but fast-moving.

Trouble was, Apple thought, it was impossible to tell if they had a tail because there was nothing to see behind save headlights. The only way to find out was to get off onto quiet roads, which meant losing time. Precious time.

Apple still had his urgency. Leaning forward over the steering-wheel, body tense, he drove as swiftly as he dared, meaning a mite just below that point at which Ethel started to shudder.

And the further trouble was, Apple gnawed, if they did have a tail, and if they shook it, the tailers could very well go back to the house in Edmonton to try to find out Ethel's destination. By then it might not matter, but Thumbs could be given a rough time of it.

From the seat behind, Sylvia said, "What're you so pensive about, Russ? I can almost hear your brain ticking."

"I'm worried about Thumbs."

"You needn't bother. So long as I'm around, she won't get you."

Apple explained, though as usual substituting gangsters for espionage operatives. He said, "I think I ought to stop at a telephone and call her. Give her a warning."

Sylvia squeezed his shoulder. "That's kind, Russ. Do it if it'll make you feel better."

Minutes later Apple drew into the kerb beside a telephone-box. On alighting from Ethel, he took note of approaching traffic. No set of headlights stopped. Which, Apple knew, didn't necessarily signify that a car hadn't stopped. Lights could have been switched off when Ethel began to slow.

In the box, its door held slightly ajar, Apple looked in the book at the legion of Morgans. Only one had an Edmonton address. He fed the coin slot, dialled, interrupted the answering voice with, "This is me—Russ."

"I *knew* I'd hear from you soon."

"No, Thumbs, nothing like that. Listen, I think you ought to know that you might—"

He, in turn, was interrupted. Thumbs said, "Can you hold on a sec, darling?"

"What?"

"There's someone at the door."

"Don't answer!" Apple shouted. "Don't open the door to anyone for any reason." He hustled through a garbled explanation about a new mob in the protection racket who were getting tough with dips.

"No perspiration," Thumbs said calmly. "I'll just show them my shotgun through the window."

"That's the way."

"And when will a certain tall gentleman with green eyes come knocking at my door, mmm?"

One of these fine days, Apple promised with his fingers crossed before he disconnected. He hurried back into Ethel. Sylvia told him that she had heard every word.

"You're great, Russ."

"So are you. Hold tight."

Apple zoomed away from the kerb. He quickly reached the tranquil point of speed; then he pressed on beyond that, reckless in his urgency. Ethel shuddered. She also began to wander off course. Apple wrestled with the wheel while wearing a smile of apology.

He was relieved on two scores—the safety of both Ethel and Sylvia—when at last he saw a sign that pointed the way to Percy's Club. He went at a reasonable speed along a track with fields on either side, topped a rise and came into a splash of brightness.

The club stood alone. It was a long, low, wooden building fronted by a veranda. With coloured light-bulbs strung everywhere possible, it looked as if it should have been on a fairground. Parked cars were spread out along this side. Behind the building was bare and dim except for a glint of water—a tributary of the Thames.

Apple brought Ethel to a stop among the cars. He and Sylvia got out. For thirty seconds they watched the rise, to see if a car appeared. None did. Apple's urgency wouldn't allow him to go on watching longer.

They went to the club and onto its veranda. There, a burly man with Percy's Club written on his sweater nodded a welcome. He told them that the floor show was due to start any minute now. It sounded as though he had been saying that for hours.

"We're reporters," Apple said. "Here to interview the Great Harold. Where could we find him, please?"

"No use asking me, mate," the man said. "The floor show's due to start any minute now."

They went inside. The room was large, its ceiling low, its ambience twilighty and smoky. The tables, three-quarters of which were taken, formed a crescent around a small dance floor. Two couples were swaying to the sludgy music made by an accordion that dwarfed its player.

From among the tables came a man in a tuxedo. He asked, "Table for two?"

Apple said, "We'd like to see the Great Harold, please."

"Of course, sir, madam. Any minute now the floor show starts. He's it."

Sylvia explained about the newspaper interview. She implied that Percy's Club was about to receive a tremendous amount of free publicity.

"Follow me, please," the headwaiter said over a bow. He led them in front of a long, busy bar, around the side of the room and to a doorway, where he left them with, "First on the right, folks."

There was a short, gloomy passage. Its end was

formed by a stack of beer-crates. The walls bore graffiti of the kind that normally made Apple cough and think of something else. Now none of the words and phrases fully registered. He rapped on the appropriate door.

It was opened by an anxious-faced man of about thirty. His hair, which reached his shoulders, was blonder than nature could produce. He wore a stage outfit of white tie and tails that had seen younger days on a fatter man.

An attempt at boredom was frustrated by hope as he asked, "Autographs, is it?"

Being gentle but firm, Apple forged his way inside, with the Great Harold backing away and Sylvia coming up behind. She closed the door.

While moving, Apple produced a monologue. In it, along with introductions, he managed to get in that he was a professional pickpocket, that he was a friend of Bellringer Alf, that he and his companion had been recommended here by Thumbs Morgan and had, in fact, been with her when she had telephoned half an hour ago.

Looking less bewildered, Harry said, "Yes, but she didn't mention . . ."

Apple winked, one tea-leaf to another. "It doesn't pay to say too much on the blower, does it, Harry?"

"Well no, you're right. I did think meself that old Thumbs sounded a bit odd."

"Cigarette, Harry?"

"Thanks. Maybe the lady would like to sit down."

Sylvia edged past the men to the narrow room's only chair. It stood by a shelf-cum-table that was full of organised mess and backed by a mirror bearing the name of a brand of chocolates. The room smelt of dampness and vinegar.

When they were all smoking, and Harry had stopped

glancing at Sylvia's white gloves, Apple explained about the travel documents which had gone missing on the day and hour stated by Thumbs Morgan.

Harry nodded. "I get the picture," he said. Absently, he produced an egg from behind his ear.

"There's a reward, I might add."

"Good, but it won't be coming to me."

Apple asked, "No documents?"

"I only made one dip that afternoon, and it wasn't off no bird. I mean lady."

"You had a poor afternoon of it then, Harry."

"I did," the Great Harold said. He blew on the egg and it turned blue. "There wasn't a decent mark around at the time, except for this one old geezer. He looked foreign and on the well-off side."

Conversationally, Apple asked, "Did you score?"

He twitched nervously as a knock battered on the door and a voice shouted, "You're on, Harry!"

"Okay!" the conjurer called. Back to a normal tone, he said, "I did score, yes, if you can call it that."

"How d'you mean?"

"Well, it wasn't much good to me."

Humming liltingly inside, Apple dropped his cigarette-end to the floor, where there were other butts, trod on it and said lightly, "So you threw away what you'd dipped, I suppose."

Harry put the blue egg behind his lapel. "Well no," he said, "as a matter of fact I didn't."

The door of the dressing-room burst open. A man looked in and snarled, "Are you deaf, Harry? For Christ's sake, man, you are *on.*"

"Okay, okay."

"These people're liable to get nasty if they're kept on the simmer."

The Great Harold bustled past Apple with a smile of apology and anxiety. "Be back soon," he said. He went out and closed the door.

Apple was going toward it and reaching for the handle until Sylvia said, "Never mind. We can wait." He stopped, turned, and blinked. Sylvia was pointing a gun at him.

She had got up from the chair. Feet apart, she stood holding the small black automatic in a central position. Her face was calm; if it did have any expression, it was one of mild interest.

Several seconds ticked by before Apple was able to speak. He asked, "Where did that thing come from?" In his surprise, he was more taken by the how than the why.

"Inside upper thigh," Sylvia said pleasantly.

"Well, well, well."

"It's a point twenty-two, by the way. A toy, some people say with contempt, but it can be lethal if you know what you're doing."

"Fine," Apple said, flopping both arms against his sides. "But what *are* you doing?"

"Making you behave yourself, Russ."

"Behave myself?"

"Making you do what I tell you to do," Sylvia said. "If you don't, I'll shoot you." She spoke so matter-of-factly that there was no doubt she meant every word.

Apple gaped. He didn't know whether he did so genuinely or as part of his act. Nor did he know if the shock he was now feeling was due to the fact that he had, apparently, been rumbled, or because Sylvia was not, after all, the straight he had so whole-heartedly believed.

Weakly he said, "This is insane."

"Yes, Russ, it's a crazy business," Sylvia said. "Put your hands together as though you were praying."

Not acting, Apple gasped, "You want me to pray?"

"Just the bit with the hands." She nudged forward her gun, which to Apple looked more obscene than it would have normally due to being inside the white glove. "Come on, Russ."

He obeyed; and again in answer to the orders that followed, he interlaced his fingers, he turned his hands so that the palms were facing the floor, he sent his arms down straight.

Sylvia said, "That's good. Don't bend your elbows, please. Now come over here and sit quietly."

"I wish to Christ I knew what this was all about. Is it a joke?"

"Drop the performance, Russ, if you don't mind. And move yourself."

Warily, his eyes fixed on the gun, Apple sidled past Sylvia and went to the chair. He sat. His clasped hands he rested on his lower thighs.

He asked, "Happy, Sylvia?"

She nodded. "I'll stay that way as long as you don't try one of those smart moves that rarely work. I don't want to shoot."

"That's nice to know."

"I wouldn't aim to kill anyway. Just cripple. But accidents can happen in a skirmish, so let's be sensible, eh?"

"Don't worry. I'm no hero, as I've told you before. I'm merely one very perplexed individual whose girl-friend has suddenly gone crackers."

"Please, Russ, let's level with each other. It's nicer that way. You know what I am and I know what you are."

"Well, at least I'm half-way there," Apple said. "I too

know what I am, but I haven't the vaguest idea what you are."

Sylvia smiled. Surprisingly, the smile seemed to hold a measure of fondness. She said, "I'm KGB, of course."

As if tasting the letters, Apple moved his lips silently. He said, "You must have the wrong initials. KGB stands for the Russian secret police."

"Really?"

Apple looked at her steadily. He asked, "Are you trying to tell me you're a Russian?"

"I certainly am."

"And that you're a *spy?*"

"Russ, you're wonderful."

Apple shook his head slowly. His shock had gone. In a strange sort of way, he was beginning to enjoy himself. His smittenship hadn't changed in intensity, it had simply shifted from the romantic to the professional. He thought with pride that he, Appleton Porter, had been in bed with this glamorous and clever Soviet agent.

"Incidentally," Sylvia said, "you were also wonderful in that cocktail lounge. You did the me-Red bit magnificently. My sincere congratulations."

"Sylvia, what exactly do you think I am?"

"Well, I didn't quite have you figured out till you made your call to Thumbs."

"But it was exactly what I said it was."

"I know."

"You mean that my call somehow gave you the impression that I'm a spy too?"

Sylvia smiled again. "No, the reverse. Almost. No spook would take the precious time out to warn someone he's only known for ten minutes. Or for ten years, come to that. The soft heart doesn't exist in this business."

"If I'm not a spy," Apple asked, "what am I?"

"An amateur. A pickpocket who was roped in to work for British Intelligence."

"But why?"

Sylvia said, "Initially, it was to go through with that obvious routine of lifting back your wallet to covertly obtain my fingerprints. Not that they'd do anyone any good. Then I suppose dear old Angus Watkin thought you might as well use the situation to make a connection with me."

That Sylvia should know of Watkin's existence came as no surprise to Apple; he didn't even dwell on it. He was busy feeling grieved about not being able to say that using the situation had been *his* idea.

He said, "This is all gibberish to me."

"Oh, sure."

"Also, I'm being insulted. You're accusing me of spying for the capitalists."

Sylvia's smile this time was a shade weary. "If you want to go on bluffing—okay. Myself, I don't mind admitting what I am, now that the game's over. Or nearly so."

"KGB, eh?"

"That's right, Russ. A Sickle, no less."

"So all that stuff you told me was a lie," Apple said. He wondered if he could live with himself if he decided that he had known it all along. No, he thought. "I believed you."

"Poor innocent Russ," Sylvia said. "That's an old trick from the shrink department. You look someone straight in the eye and tell him an absolute truth. After that he tends to believe everything you say. It helps even more if you can throw in some additional truths."

"What truths are you talking about?"

"I told you I have to wear gloves because of allergies. That is one hundred per cent correct. It's also true that I had lessons in picking pockets, but they were from a master at the art, not a school friend. And I wasn't lying when I said that I didn't know what the missing item was."

Again Apple shook his head slowly. "You don't even know what you're looking for?"

"You're a sticker, Russ, I'll say that for you. But it's another sign of the amateur. The pro would've fessed up by now, to see what he could learn by telling."

"I couldn't learn what you don't know yourself."

"But come to think of it," Sylvia said, ignoring him, "if you're being used by Angus Watkin, it isn't likely that he'd tell you much. He's known to be a close one, even with his real agents."

"Why couldn't I be a real agent?"

"Too nice. Too tall."

Apple said, "You realise, of course, that we're missing the floor show."

Ignoring that also, Sylvia said, "So I'll spoil Watkin's fun by telling you what half the spooks in London seem to know. Which is that all this concerns a man from the Soviet Embassy called Narkov. He was dipped of a mystery item before dropping dead on a platform of Piccadilly underground station."

"At three-thirty last Thursday," Apple said. "It's brilliant of me to guess that."

"Narkov had been under observation for some weeks on his afternoons off."

"By the KGB?" Apple said. "But you just told me he was a Russian."

Blandly, Sylvia asked, "You mean he wasn't passing information to the Brits?"

"If you think I know anything about anything in this deal, you're crazy."

"But as I was saying. We have films of Narkov going to

various business places. We have a film of him sitting in a park. We have a film of him getting his shoes polished. We even have a film of a Brit agent filming Narkov."

"That's a heap of movie-making."

"The best of the lot, however, is a close-up of you and me making love," Sylvia said, as easily as though she meant washing dishes. "Anyway, it appears obvious that Comrade Narkov . . ."

Her words faded from Apple's awareness. He was stricken, both by the blush he could feel speedily approaching and by the news that had given it birth. He had been filmed while performing the sex act.

The blush rampaged up Apple's neck. It burned across his face like a bush fire. His freckles disappeared. The physical heat and emotional discomfort were torture. Apple thought it must be the worst attack of his life.

Breaking off in mid-sentence, Sylvia leaned forward to say a hesitant, "Russ?"

Sitting stiff, his straight arms rigid, Apple tried to remember his latest short-term cure for blushing. He couldn't. Nor could he recall any of the old ones. His mind was too occupied with reviving details of himself and Sylvia on the bed.

"Are you all right, Russ?"

Apple gasped, "What?"

Sylvia backed slowly away. Alarm in her face and voice, she said, "You've gone a terrible red. You look as if you're going to explode."

"Who?" He didn't know what he was saying. The blushing attack raged on.

"You haven't swallowed a pill or something, have you?" Sylvia asked, still reversing worriedly. "You look really odd." She came to a stop by the door.

It opened.

SIX

Everything happened quickly.

The door, coming open with a rush, hit Sylvia hard in the back. She jerked forward, her arms spreading.

Apple got up swiftly from his chair. The blush was still on his face but not in his mind.

Harry began to come in.

Partly off balance, Sylvia swung around.

Apple strode forward.

Harry saw the gun. He blanched, whirled like a gifted dancer, and ran.

Sylvia began to turn back towards her hostage.

Apple brought down a chopping blow on the automatic. It fell from Sylvia's grip and hit the floor. The clatter was still sounding as, using both hands for full force, Apple swept Sylvia back behind him. There was more clatter as she fell over with the chair.

Not wasting time by grabbing for the gun, Apple went dashing out. He hit the passage wall, caromed off sideways and shot on to the doorway and came out into the main room.

The scene was as before, except for more couples dancing, and for people at nearby tables looking behind them. The localised attraction was Harry. He stood by the bar, gabbling worriedly at the headwaiter.

Loping forward, Apple realised that his blush had faded. With exhilaration it occurred to him that by accident he might have discovered the ultimate short-term cure for his affliction: abrupt action. A shock, in fact, in the style of that which was used to cure hiccoughs. He would have to give it some serious thought.

"A gun?" the headwaiter asked loudly.

After which, he and the Great Harold looked around. They saw Apple approaching at speed. Harry threw himself into a flying start in the other direction. The headwaiter leapt at the bar, vaulted it with legs wildly akimbo —and dropped out of sight.

He was imitated in the disappearance act by two bartenders and a glass-washer. People at close tables were getting up or twisting about to look in all directions. A man on a high stool at the bar, he began to fall backwards.

Apple was vaguely aware of shoving him upright again as he passed by the spot, at the same time calling out, "Listen, Harry! Wait! Listen!"

The conjurer, it seemed, would not have waited for that more renowned Harry, Houdini (whose real name, Apple recalled in fleet passing, had been Erich Weiss). He raced on to the club's entrance.

There, newcomers were crowding in, most of them tipsy and boisterous. The Great Harold tried to get through. He was prevented from doing so because, apparently, the people took his white-tie outfit to mean that he was the headwaiter.

They were all around him and calling for a table for six when Apple arrived at that point. Seeing his pursuer, Harry fought his way out, though not on the door side.

As he staggered on around the room, up behind him flew a pack of playing cards. It broke apart and its members floated like generous ticker-tape.

With cards bouncing off his head, Apple glanced

back. Sickle Sylvia was coming from the dressing-room passage. She had a limp. Her gun was nowhere to be seen.

Naturally, Apple mused in relief. Your true-blue pro operatives never drew attention to themselves in public, even with an umbrella, let alone a gun.

Pushing hard, but mumbling beg-pardons, Apple quickly made his way through the newcomers, over whom he towered. A woman snarled at him to mind where he put his filthy giraffe paws. He swept on.

Harry was at an emergency door. He pulled fiercely on the bar that bore a PUSH label. His face was contorted with fear and frustration, his overlarge suit was doing a dance of a different style.

The Great Harold saw Apple. Giving up on the door, he began to back away, at the same time delivering a frantic bombardment. His aim was poor.

Apple had no trouble dodging the eggs, a snuff-box, two fans and another float of playing cards. He felt smooth. When a bunch of plastic flowers came flying at him, he grabbed it and tossed it back.

He said, "Listen to me, Harry."

"Leave me alone!" the conjurer yelled.

"I'm on your side."

Harry threw an object that had the appearance of a black plate. As Apple hit it with a deflecting hand, it popped out into a top hat.

Startled by that, Apple's rugby tackle was wide of the mark. He flew by Harry, hit the ground and rolled. He rolled against the legs of a man, who promptly came down on top of him. Apple, wrestling himself free, leapt up with a muttered "Terribly sorry."

There was now a growing uproar in the room. Most patrons at the outer tables were standing. Some were heading for the door. The dwarfed accordionist had upped his tempo to fast jig-time. Sylvia was lost in the crowd.

Apple jumped over the man he had brought down and ran on. He was elated: stirred by the chase, excited by thoughts of being the one who would get the coveted item, thrilled by the way he had cleverly outwitted a gun-toting pro agent.

Harry, his long blond hair flopping, was forging his way through standers at tables. Some people snatched at him with worried questions. Some laughed at him ner-vously, not sure if this was a new kind of encore.

Apple closed in. He became one of the snatchers. Repeatedly, his fingers scraped off the Great Harold's shoulder. He hissed that he was trying to help while part-answering the worriers and grinning at the laughers.

Harry kept moving. He twisted and turned with a skill that suggested this wasn't the first time he had made an escape through a crowd.

It occurred to Apple suddenly that Sylvia could be making her way across from the other side, and thus meet Harry face-on. The situation turned urgent-plus. Apple lunged.

His fingers again failed to get a grip on the shoulder, but, in swooping low from his lunge, he made contact with the jacket's tails. He grabbed and held on.

Harry was jerked to a stop. That lasted only a blink of time. With a fast shrug, the conjurer slipped out of his coat. It sprang backwards.

From pockets known and secret flew various objects: a stuffed rabbit, coloured balls, several rubbery bananas, two green roses and, finally, a real-looking serpent six feet long.

At sight of the last, nearby women screamed. There

was a rush to leave the vicinity, despite some people laughing that the thing was imitation.

The way was thus rendered less congested for Apple. Speedily, he went on. He came up right behind Harry. This time he didn't try to do any restraining, which, he realised, had been the wrong psychological move.

In a chatty tone, bending like a forgiving teacher, he said, "I'll get you away from here."

With a violent twist of his body Harry looked back and up. "Christ," he gasped.

"Steady, Harry."

The magician lurched off backwards. "Don't shoot!"

Apple waggled his hands in the air. "See, no gun. She's after me as well. I'm going to get you away from her."

He had raised his voice, the din growing and Harry moving, but his words still had no effect. The Great Harold went off between tables, a V of red galluses bright against his tired white shirt.

A man poked himself into Apple's path, asking with a whoosh of whisky breath, "Did someone shoot a snake?"

"Yes," Apple said, elbowing by. "It's dead. The panic's over. Sit down." He hurried on towards the dance floor.

Harry was there, trying to get through the couples who, with faces of uncertainty, were jerking to the jig-time beat. The orchestra had made himself even smaller; only his eyes and the top of his head showed above the accordion.

About half the people in the club were now standing. Some applauded. The question of what was going on batted around over various answers relating to dead snakes.

Apple reached the dancers. He began to thread his

way through. So as not to be too noticeable, he sagged at the knees springily in rhythm with the jig.

In the middle of the dance floor, Harry was attempting to get away from a woman. She wanted him to dance with her. His face was distraught and his hair was dangling in sweat-gummed hanks.

Apple threaded on bobbingly. He reached the conjurer, who began to yawn with terror as Apple, polite yet firm, moved the dance-mad woman aside. He went around Harry and started to back away, saying: "Follow me. You'll be all right. I can get you away from these gangsters." He beckoned assuringly with both hands. "Come on, Harry."

Dazedly, his mouth half-agape, the Great Harold came forward in a hesitant sideways movement. He asked, "What?"

"Trust me, Harry."

"Gangsters?"

His voice raised because of the clamour, stooping forward as he continued to reverse, Apple explained in brief about the protection racket that was being worked on pickpockets.

"You'll be all right with me, Harry."

The conjurer, nodding, looked partly convinced. He started to make better speed, but then Apple got blocked on coming off the dance floor. Every patron was standing, filling the paths between tables.

Apple remembered the serpent. You're brilliant, he told himself while shouting "Mice!"

It took three additional shouts, each one accompanied by more silence than the last, before there was a response. Then it was general. Squealing, women began to climb up on the chairs and tables. Some men did the same.

The paths became less clogged. Taking Harry's arm, Apple led him along. They went slowly at first but faster as more and more people made it up from the floor.

The squealing went on. Apple was fascinated to see that all the women held their skirts in the same way, as though it had been taught to them in school.

Patrons were leaving densely through the main door. Once clear of the tables, Apple took Harry past it and on to the emergency exit, which was open now. People were passing out in a thin stream.

Until the penultimate second, Apple failed to notice the three men who stood quietly beside the exit. It was only as he was about to go through, with Harry, that he saw, and recognised at once, the three Cubans.

The nearest gave Apple a fierce shove in the chest. He went careening backwards. He stumbled and fell flat. By the time he sat up, it was to see the three Cubans hurriedly leaving, taking Harry with them.

Apple leapt to his feet.

After skirmishing around several people, Apple gained the door. He was delayed by the slow exiting of a chubby couple. Twitching, he pressed on behind. At last he got through. Outside, more people were gathered, like spectators at a real good disaster.

There was also vehicular movement. Some cars were leaving, most were arriving. Lights flashed and horns blasted. The ambience crackled with tension.

Apple saw the four men. They were moving along a lane between parked cars. Progress was slow, since the three in dark suits needed to force along the one who stood out because of his white shirt.

Apple gave chase.

He decided to speed up in the rear quietly, make a

surprise attack. This started off well, and looked like coming off, the gap closing between himself and the group, but then one of the Cubans glanced back.

In Spanish, he shouted a warning that the long one was coming. His colleagues hurried on with Harry as the shouter turned to supply rearguard action.

Charging in without finesse or a battle design, Apple recognised the man as the one he had code-named Macho. Bald pate giving off a shine, he stood waiting in the correct crouch of unarmed combat.

They met with a crash, the irresistible force and the immovable object. Theory was proven right in that an explosion occurred. They burst away from each other and fell back untidily against cars.

Macho was the first to reassemble himself. He came forward snarling like a giant chihuahua. His right-hander to the eyes skidded past Apple's ear. His left crunched on a rib.

Apple doubled over with a grunt. He clutched the man in a stooping bear-hug. They tussled in gasping silence, heaving to and fro, pushing back and forth.

A man and woman appeared, walking arm in arm. Turning neatly on sighting the battlers, they went off in another direction with a muttered comment about bloody idiots. Obviously, differences being settled in the car park was no novelty at Percy's Club.

Macho flung himself free of the bear-hug. When he came in again, it was with his forearms going like fast metronomes. But that was a diversion. Apple didn't see the high kick while it was on its way; he only felt the pain as a shoe clunked on his breastbone.

In instinctively grabbing both hands towards the place of damage, Apple touched an ankle. He took a firm hold on it and, with all his strength, wrenched upward. He didn't let go until the bald man's other foot was far above the ground.

Macho sailed away as though he were floating through a backward somersault. There was a loud, metallic thud as his head made flush contact with the side of a car; a muffled bump as he landed on the ground; a small groan as he rolled limply onto his side.

If Apple had been acting in accordance with the instructions he had been given in Training Three, he would have delivered a sharp kick to the underside of the man's jaw. He couldn't bring himself to do that. In any case, he knew it wasn't necessary: Macho would be out of action for minutes to come.

Apple ran on in pursuit.

His height, coupled with bounding leaps, enabled him to see over the crowd of parked vehicles. He picked out a moving patch of white. It and two dark patches were ahead, in a parallel lane between cars.

Quickly, Apple caught up. Stooping, he drew level and then went further on. Crafty, he crept between parked vehicles. Tense, he stopped and waited.

The three men came huffing along. The Cubans had Harry between them, one towing and one pushing. In Spanish they were urging each other to make haste. The conjurer looked to be in a state of shock.

The men came level. Apple abruptly shot up to his full six feet seven inches and flung his arms high and gave an ear-blasting Samurai yell.

Gasping their startlement noisily, the three men broke step. Harry almost fell. The leader was dragging him upright as Apple threw himself forward. The other Cuban leapt to intercept. They met and tangled.

Aware that the leader was hustling the conjurer away, Apple busily blocked blows and sent over some of his own, which were blocked as well. It was all as neat and standard as in a gymnasium.

Then the Cuban made a move that was both surprising and unorthodox. Using his comparative shortness to advantage, he bent swiftly and dodged under the attacking-defending arms. He slammed a shoulder into Apple's midriff, clasped him by the waist and heaved upward.

Apple went over like a bag of feathers. He came down like a sack of cement. Breath wheezed out of him as he hit the ground, landing on his back. Every bone in his body jangled and every muscle twanged.

But he was quick to remember the kick, the one which he himself couldn't deliver. He was ready even before he saw it coming at him.

Rather than deflection, it was avoidance that Apple chose as possibly being the most useful here. So he merely dodged his head.

The kicking foot went past, and on, and up. The Cuban lost his balance. Arms windmilling, he stumbled backwards. Only by grabbing hold of a driving mirror in skimming along the car it was attached to did he hold himself from falling.

He assumed, apparently (Apple still being on his back) that the fight was over, for he turned away and began to run. Apple was up fast. Again he tried a rugby tackle. This time he made it. His dive through space ended with his arms around the Cuban's legs. He brought his man down.

Quickly, Apple scrambled forward on all fours until he was able to sit on the small of the man's back. He clasped his hands, raised them high, and, wincing, brought the grip down hard. It landed solidly in the nape of the neck. The Cuban slumped unconscious.

Apple jumped up, ran on. Two down and one to go,

he mused as he began to take great bounds. The ploy supplied no clue to the pair he sought. He stopped running and climbed up on top of a car. Its roof dented with a sad clunk.

There were moving cars and people in all directions, with more headlights approaching from the highway. Patrons were still leaving the club building and others were trying to go inside.

On his second scan around the area, just as people were beginning to notice him on top of the car, and point, Apple saw a gleam of flopping yellow. It was Harry's hair.

Apple clambered down without style, not caring to take a chance on a buccaneer leap. Even so, he stumbled in the new darkness below. He recovered and set out on a twisting run through the maze of lanes between vehicles.

On reaching the edge of the parking area, with the river nearby, Apple saw that the Great Harold was struggling with his captor, who was cursing in a furious mumble. Silk scarves were drooling from the conjurer's hip pocket.

Apple sprang between the two men. Pushing the Cuban back, he told Harry, "Don't worry, it's all over."

"Thank God."

"Just step aside."

Harry obeyed, more or less; he moved but not on foot. After slapping down to a sit, as though all strength had gone from his legs, he began to rumper his way backwards. This Apple noted only vaguely, being now engaged in warding off a flurry of blows from the leader Cuban.

A car turned this way. Its headlights were up and dazzling. They caught the Cuban in the face. He ducked. As he did, Apple brought down a karate chop on the side of his neck. The man sagged. Bending, he closed in and embraced Apple's waist.

The car went on slowly by, with one voice from inside calling encouragement and another saying shame on two grown men for acting like that.

In dimness again, Apple went on trying to shake free of the remaining Cuban, who was dazed but knew exactly how to protect himself. He held on around the waist while being swung mightily from side to side.

Another car turned onto the scene. It slowed and then stopped. Wondering if he should ask for help, and knowing he wouldn't do anything of the kind, Apple looked around.

He saw a figure, dim behind the headlights, get out and open the rear door. He heard the figure say, the voice female, "This way. You're safe now." He saw Harry get up and go towards the car, which he recognised at the same moment as he remembered the woman's voice.

The Mayflowers had arrived.

Furious, Apple wrenched his body fro and forth. The Cuban maintained his hold. He continued to do so even when he lost his footing, which worsened the situation for Apple by tugging him into a stoop.

He gasped, "Stop." It was meant for those at the car, but it had no effect. Harry got in the back, falling more than boarding normally. The woman followed him inside and slammed the door.

The large blue Daimler, the same car that had nearly run Apple down in Soho, started to reverse. It went from sight beyond parked vehicles.

Desperate, enraged at being bested again by the lean, tanned couple, Apple took a firm grip on the semidead-weight Cuban and began to turn in a circle. It was slow going at first, but he quickly picked up speed.

The man's legs left the ground. They moved out until he was stretched horizontal in the air. Apple went on twirling. His vision became a jumble of speeding lights. He wondered how long he could go on.

Just as Apple was about to end this circling and try a more lethal tactic, the Cuban lost his grip. He went flying free, hit the ground and bounced to a stop. The groan he gave stated articulately that he was throwing in the towel.

Apple's vision was still swirling. His legs plaited and he almost tripped himself up. That corrected, he started to walk. He reeled drunkenly. When this began to ease off, he saw that he was going the wrong way.

He ran back.

Rounding the pack of stationary vehicles, Apple spotted the Daimler. Behind another car, which dictated its speed, it was moving slowly across the track away from the club.

Tensing forward on the balls of his feet, Apple debated if he should try to catch up running, which was not inconceivable, or if he should go to the other side of the parking area and get Ethel, which would waste a precious minute.

He was still undecided when the Daimler cut off onto a side track, escaping the lumbering car in front. Speeding up, it went toward a wooden bridge with a humpback.

Apple lost his hesitancy. He was running off in a parallel direction even before he had finished telling himself that the bridge led only to the club's picnic island; that with luck he could be there before the CIA pair; that with even greater luck he could run some kind of interference.

Apple sped across an open stretch of lawn. It ended in

a sharp line, beyond which lay a darkness with glints, like sequins on black velvet.

Having been here before, Apple knew not only the layout but also the vital details, such as depth. Therefore he slowed not a fraction on nearing the river bank. He went straight from a run into a headlong dive.

Apple's flesh shrieked as he hit the water. It was autumn cold. Even if he hadn't been in a hurry, he would have wanted to stay there as briefly as possible. He was already doing the crawl when he surfaced from his shallow dive.

Another spur that kept Apple at full-pressure swimming was the thought of Harry sitting in the back of the Daimler with Ms. Mayflower. Not waiting until they got clear of this danger area, she could already be asking about the missing item.

Apple churned through the water rapidly. Except for lifts to breathe after every third right-arm stroke, he kept his face in the water; he didn't want to lose important seconds by looking up to see how he was doing or how far the Daimler had progressed.

One hand touched bottom. Next, Apple was wading. Above him loomed the trees which covered most of the one-acre island. Between trunks to his left he could see intermittent flashes from a single set of headlights.

Reaching the bank, Apple heaved himself up. He took turns at panting and shivering as he lurched through the trees. Enough light came from the brightness across the river for him to see with fair clarity. All around lay the sodden oddments of a picnic area out of season.

Apple came to a path. The only one with sufficient width to be used by vehicles, it circled the island's outer edge. His breathing having become normal, Apple only shivered as he stood in uncertainty. What should he do next?

Get out of sight, to begin with, he told himself. The Daimler was approaching, its lights swinging up and down as the car swept over the uneven dirt path.

Apple charged across into the trees at the other side. Forming a vague plan, he went straight on. If only they could see me now, he enjoyed thinking, even though he didn't know whom he meant exactly by *they*.

A prop palm tree, a shabby South Seas hut, barbecue pits and rustic furniture—these flashed past as Apple went on, loping rather than racing because of the reduced visibility here away from the club's brightness. The Daimler was to his rear, circling the island. He didn't have much time.

With his feeble, emergency strategy formed, Apple came to the path at the island's far side. He looked around for usable material. Best seemed to be a large picnic table, with benches attached on either side.

Apple took it by one end. He started to drag it, to cover the fifteen feet to the path. But the table was solid, heavy. Progress was slow and the headlights of the Daimler were growing less flickery. Apple strained with all his might. He stopped shivering.

It wasn't going to happen, Apple accepted when for the second time a leg of the table caught on a root. There was still six or eight feet to go.

An upswing of the headlights gave Apple a clue. He dashed to the table's other end, stooped, grabbed a cross-bar and lifted. When the table was standing on its end, he pushed it over, grinning.

Again Apple heaved the table up. He shoved it over. Now it was far enough on the path to form a barrier.

A moment before the Daimler's lights swept cleanly

into view, Apple flung himself flat. He crawled away in the undergrowth, stopping when he was out of sight. He peered back towards the path.

The large blue car came to a halt, reluctantly and peevishly. Over the genteel hum of its engine could be heard a masculine "We needed this." The accent wasn't the British one the man had used in Soho.

He alighted from the car swiftly, went forward into the headlights' glare and began to push at the table.

Rising with caution, Apple set off quietly in the opposite direction. He circled at a creep to the car's rear. Ms. Mayflower and Harry were silhouetted in the back window. The conjurer was on the right.

Which is the side Apple went to now, walking in a waddly squat. The woman called out to her partner to hurry and he asked her what the hell she thought he was trying to do.

Apple drew abreast of the rear door. Since any diversion, no matter how small, is better than no diversion at all, he picked up a stone and threw it over the roof of the car. As a clatter sounded in the far undergrowth, he acted.

In the same fast movement, Apple rose to his feet and yanked open the door. Ms. Mayflower was peering through the other window towards where the stone had fallen. By the time she looked around, Apple had reached inside and grabbed Harry by the shirt.

"Out!" Apple snapped.

Luckily, the conjurer responded like a greyhound to the opening trap. Although he still looked to be in a state of shock, he lurched toward Apple, who pulled him out with one hand and then with the other slammed the door. Its closed window bonged loudly on the brow of Ms. Mayflower, who had acted promptly to follow. She fell back.

Her partner had darted from the table. As Apple dragged Harry into the trees, the male CIA agent was approaching at speed. But his attacking charge ended abruptly. On leaving the headlights' glare, he halted. He had been blinded by the sudden change to darkness.

Pulling Harry on through the trees, Apple asked, "You can swim, can't you?"

With the shrill edge of hysteria in his voice, the Great Harold said, "No, I can't. I won't."

"Okay, don't worry."

"I'm not going near no water."

"Forget it, Harry. No one's swimming."

Looking back as they ran parallel to the path, Apple saw that both Mayflowers were moving towards the picnic-table barrier, male with agility, female at a slower pace and with a hand to her brow.

So as not to think about that, feel guilty, Apple turned his mind to what the American couple might be planning, since they obviously had no intentions of giving chase on foot. He decided that they would block off the island's only solid exit, the bridge.

Knowing better than to expect to find a boat conveniently tied up somewhere at hand, Apple hurried the conjurer closer to the path. Onto it as they moved along, part in the glare, he tossed whatever he could find.

Chairs there were, and crates of empty bottles, also two thick logs and a barrel. The most gratifying of all, however, was another heavy table. It was right beside the path on its other side.

Midway across, holding onto Harry with one hand, Apple noted that the headlights were moving. What made him pay closer attention was that the limousine's motor seemed to be racing at top power. He then saw that only one of the headlights was working. Also, the Daimler appeared to be weaving without trouble in and out of the thrown objects.

That, Apple knew, was impossible. But he didn't connect the revving engine, the single light and that weaving with a motor cycle until he saw one, until the machine came roaring over the final yards.

That Apple did connect the motor cycle with Watkin's people was the reason he stood on there, took no evasive action.

But this was not the arrival of help, Apple soon realised. It was a kidnap.

There were two men on the bike. The one behind was the bag-snatcher. What he snatched this time was Harry. As the motor cycle went by he reached out and jerked the conjurer off his feet.

Turning, Apple watched them go. He stood slack, dazed, his features loose. He felt like a police constable who arrests a widely sought, infamous criminal, and then has him taken away by a detective, who will get the glory. He felt abused and insulted.

Less dazed, more piqued, Apple nevertheless reasoned with himself that he had, after all, been ordered to stay out of this part of the caper, that Angus Watkin had said his other people would work at finding the mystery pickpocket. So he had no real grounds for complaint.

Reason having been allowed its say, Apple started walking in the direction taken by the motor cycle. Next, he was striding. Last, he broke into a run.

Apple was not going to stand for the snatch. Brits or no Brits, he had done the finding and he had every right to wear the laurel wreath, to mention nothing of cocking a snoot at Angus Watkin.

The motor cycle had covered only some fifty yards.

Chugging, it swayed along strainingly with the weight of its three passengers. The bag-snatcher (who had been responsible for that crack on the hand, Apple wasn't forgetting) held Harry half across his shoulders.

Running steadily and grimly, gaining, Apple spared a thought for the Mayflowers. They, he reckoned, would give up now. Their assumption would be that the prized dip was lost to them, secure in the custody of three British agents.

Except that the pair ahead probably weren't full-blown operatives, Apple mused. More likely they were faceless ones whose speciality was motor cycle gimmickry. As such, they would be easier to deal with.

He was catching up. The bike was thirty yards on. Harry was gazing back, limply resigned, but he did flap a hand in response when Apple waved.

The weaving motor cycle went down a dip in the path, which caused it to veer more severely off course. The three passengers teetered to one side. It was only the driver's skill that held them aboard, as well as keeping the machine from colliding with a tree.

His body warm inside the sodden clothes, Apple ran on at his stable pace. He was making no schemes of how to deal with the two men, but did think that when (not if) he got them out of his way, he could use their bike to escape with Harry.

Gaining more, Apple realised that he had surprise on his side: the pair of Brits didn't know he was behind: driver unable to see him via the rear-view mirror because he was no longer in the Daimler's headlights, rider unable to look behind because of his human burden.

Apple put on speed. That, plus the fact that the motor bike had started tacking, reduced the gap rapidly. Harry watched the approach with torpid interest.

Apple came abreast of the machine's rear. Still without a plan, he simply made a grab at Harry. The conjurer lost his torpidity. Jerking himself away he yelled, "I'll fall!"

Which noisy action caused the bag-snatcher to swing his head around. He made a pushing motion towards Apple and shouted, "Go back, you idiot!"

"Idiot yourself," Apple snarled. He clutched the pushing hand—hard, to return in a small way the unfavour of damage.

He held the grip, the driver surged ahead, Apple was jerked off his feet. He hit the ground. For a distance of three yards and a time of five seconds, Apple was towed, the machine reared like a nervy horse, the Brits cursed, and the Great Harold yelled in fear.

Apple freed his hand. He slumped to a stop on the path, coughing at dust. For a moment he lay there, supporting his chin on a hand and watching the motor cycle draw away. It looked to be making better time.

Gritting his teeth, Apple jumped up. He started to give chase. But he soon discovered that the crest of his power had been spent. He couldn't get going in top kick. The struggling, running, fighting and swimming had all charged their toll.

The gap between himself and the motor cycle stayed constant at about twenty yards. It seemed so short a distance, yet he was unable to make it shrink no matter how hard he tried. He did manage to chop off a yard by short-cutting a bend in the path, but then the motor cycle not only got that bit back, it began to gain more.

They were out of the trees now and on smoother going. The humpback bridge lay ahead. Without the slightest hope, but not allowing himself to give in, Apple pounded on in tired pursuit. He noted with indifference that calm had returned over at the club.

The motor cycle continued to draw away. It went
onto the approach to the bridge. Apple was questioning
the sense in keeping up his losing chase, drearily, when he
saw that the motor bike had started to zigzag. It was, in
stimulating fact, going at a creep.

Apple sprang forward with renewed vigour. The
overloaded bike, he realised, was having trouble making
it up the incline to the crown of the bridge's hump.

The gap shrank like ice in a furnace. Apple was running hard and the motor cycle was moving at a walking
pace, as well as tacking in heavy lurches. One swing
brought it dangerously close to the wooden parapet.

With his spirits rising, Apple arrived on the bridge. Its
boards boomed to his footfalls. He had to labour hard to
fight the ascent; but he reached the roaring, straining
motor cycle just before it got to the summit.

Harry had been watching with stark concern. Now he
drew back violently. This shift of balance caused the
driver to steer around, which brought the motor cycle
into an almost side-on position to Apple.

His response was immediate, which gave a boost to
his rising spirits. He shot out both arms, his hands up and
flat. The strong pushes landed right, on the shoulders of
the two Brits, who went falling sideways. All three men
came off the machine, which then fell itself.

For a moment, there was three-way wrestling on the
boards. The Great Harold whimpered to God and the
Brits swore at Apple. These vocals were extended when,
striding over the motor cycle, Apple shoved the uppermost of the Brits down on top of the other, and, in the next
movement, yanked Harry roughly to his doddery feet.

"Run!" he hissed. He turned the conjurer in the right
direction and pushed him on his way.

Swinging back, Apple found the uppermost man

crouched in the act of rising. The kick Apple threw was meant for the place where it would do least damage while having an immediate effect: the belly.

The aim was perfect. Gasping, the snatcher went over backwards. He curled himself into a foetal ball and rolled across to the bike.

"You f—— maniac," the other man raged, scrambling aside. He leapt up.

"You thieving bastard," Apple said. He moved forward at the same moment as the man attacked, and realised that he had guessed right in respect of faceless ones: the man had only basic knowledge of dirty fighting.

He threw a boxer's neat left. It was aimed at the groin. Apple slapped it down. He grabbed the man's hair and jerked him upright, let go suddenly, squatted and grasped him around the hips.

With a whine of effort, Apple rose. It took a lot of his remaining strength to do that, and still more to stagger over to the parapet.

From there on it was easy. Being tall, Apple didn't need to lift. He simply put the struggling Brit on top of the parapet and let him go. The man fell over with a yell, which ended after a splash.

Apple trundled on across the bridge. His legs were weak. Topping the crown, he saw Harry weaving as he went down the slope. Apple pushed forward into a descent-eased trot in order to catch up.

"Come on," he panted, taking Harry's arm. The conjurer mentioned God.

Like the halt leading the lame, they went off the bridge and onto the track that led over the open field. Apple kept urging speed with tugs. Harry responded so well that Apple added the verbal.

"Quick as you can," he said—and stopped dead. He stared along the track.

Ethel was coming.

For one electrifying, insane moment, Apple thought that the ex-taxi-cab was coming by herself—to help.

Then Apple saw through the blur of headlights that there was a driver. The dark shape's identity was given away by white hands on the steering-wheel.

Abruptly, Ethel surged forward. She was coming straight at Apple and Harry. Taking the conjurer with him, Apple leapt out of the way.

They made it with inches to spare. Apple was struggling to hold them both upright when he heard the squeal-grind of cruel braking. Balance regained, he wincingly turned.

Ethel stood nearby with dust rising around her. Leaning through the window was Sylvia. Her outstretched arm pointed the small automatic. She said, "Russ, you stay there. Harry, come and get in."

Before Apple could even begin to think how to handle this situation, the conjurer moved away. His eyes were intent on the gun. He was deaf to Apple's "Listen. Wait."

"Quiet, Russ," Sylvia said, her voice calm. "It won't do any good. And if you try anything . . ."

Apple came close to saying, "You won't get away with this." He had always wanted to. But he was too tired and emotionally spent to offer an argument. He shrugged.

Fearful-meek, Harry got in the back of the retired taxi and closed the door. He collapsed onto the seat and disappeared from view.

Sylvia took Ethel forward. Her gun still aimed, steering one-handed, she turned the steering-wheel to circle where Apple stood. He himself circled to keep her in sight. As she went by and off into the straight, Sylvia smiled.

That did it.

The smile.

It was a gloat, a victor's smirk, a blasé insult added to unfair injury, a raspberry for the loser.

The smile galvanised Apple into action.

Using power that he didn't know he still had, Apple tore after the ex-taxi-cab. Within seconds he caught up. He took a mighty jump. His left foot landed on the rear bumper, his right hand grasped the roof-rack. He was firmly on.

That Sylvia knew about his presence was shown by the way Ethel suddenly swerved. Apple was flung into a sideways whiplash. He managed to hold on and had just recovered when it happened again, in the other direction. He still held on.

Apple realised, however, that his position was tenuous. He could be shaken off with more swerves or by bumpy going, which Sylvia would create or find so as to get rid of him.

The reason she didn't stop and order him away at gunpoint, Apple knew, was because there was always the chance of him getting control of the gun. Also, she wanted to leave this place where there were so many others after the same prize.

Once again Apple's height came in useful. He had no trouble pulling himself up on the roof-rack. Within seconds he was kneeling on the top of Ethel.

Who suddenly made another swerve. Apple grabbed on in time, but he still almost went over with his lower body. On getting straight again, he jammed his feet against the rear bar of the roof-rack, as well as maintaining a double grip on its front.

It was clever of Sylvia, Apple acknowledged, to have waited before doing that last swerve. She was, in fact, a right worthy opponent. Unfortunately.

They left the area of Percy's Club and came onto the main highway. It was medium busy with traffic. Sylvia started to speed up. Apple had to slit his eyes against the increasing strength of the wind.

Ethel passed a car. After zipping around a corner, she began to overtake a bus. Its passengers gazed with dull, doubting eyes at Apple as he went steadily by the windows. He pretended not to notice.

Bus passed, the road ahead was open. Ethel went faster. She quickly reached the point where she was trembling at the punishment. On account of his tight hold, Apple trembled right along, like a man with a road-drill.

So as not to think about falling off, Apple wondered if, when a slow patch came, he should whip off his jacket and lower it over the windshield. No, he decided; he couldn't hold both his coat and the roof-rack at the same time.

Roadside trees appeared. Apple hoped they wouldn't give Sickle Sylvia the idea of knocking him off the top by finding a tree with low branches.

Ethel slowed. She was coming to a traffic island. It was small and empty of traffic. Speeding up again, the ex-taxi-cab went onto the island and began to circle it. The speed rose, the circling continued.

Apple found that, due to centrifugal pressure, he was being forced over to the outer side. Gradually, his right arm became straight and taut. Unable to send strength through his legs, he felt his shoes start to lose their traction against the bar.

The circle tightened. Ethel swayed far over. For a hellish, sickening second, Apple thought she was going to fall. Her bodywork would be ruined.

Without warning, Ethel not only straightened out but, turning off the traffic island, she swung the other way.

Apple was whipped in that direction. He went partly onto his back and one leg waved out over the edge. But he kept his place, and the next moment Ethel was running level again.

And at a normal speed. Here, in a residential area, there was more traffic. Apple used the respite to relax and to try working out a plan.

He thought that if he climbed down at the side, using the running-board to stand on, he could lean inside and force Sylvia to stop by some kind of interference. She wasn't likely to attempt to use her automatic. Guns had a habit of shooting their possessors in close fumbles.

Apple edged over to the side rail of the roof-rack. He was pleased with his plotting. He fancied the idea of himself standing on the running-board of a speeding vehicle. He could see it now.

The residential street was turning into a commercial road, while also getting broader. There being ample room for cars to overtake, Apple told himself that he had better act quickly, before Sylvia got back to top speed.

But, Apple realised with surprise, Ethel was slowing, rather than the reverse.

This went on and Ethel herself began to be passed by other cars. From one of these came shouts, asking where the circus was playing.

Apple, seeing that Ethel was going so slowly that a halt in the kerb seemed certain, got tensely ready for action, though he didn't know what form it would take.

Trouble was, Apple suspected that Sylvia, rather than risk being dropped down on if she got out, would peer her gun over the roof's edge.

Ethel drew to a stop in the side of the road. She was

neatly parked. The headlights went off, the hand-brake ratched on, the engine died. There then followed a pause of silence and stillness.

Tense, Apple waited.

The driver's door, which was at the other side, swung slowly open.

Apple acted. Swiftly, he got over the far edge. He clambered down to Ethel's roadway side. Snatching open the rear door he reached inside. His grab at Harry made it only midway. He stopped on seeing Sylvia through the windows.

She was some yards distant. Tugging in competent fashion at the cuff of a glove, Sickle Sylvia strolled away towards the nearest building. It was a station of the underground railway system. She moved as though she had hours to spare.

Tension oozed out of Apple like sap from a snapped flower stem. He had the awful suspicion that he was about to be disappointed.

Apple read Sylvia's manner as telling of philosophical acceptance. When, before going into the station entrance, the Sickle turned with a wave, Apple returned it glumly.

Sylvia gone from sight, Apple sighed and gave his attention to the man on the seat. The Great Harold was slumped with his eyes closed.

He whispered, "I'll never be the same again."

Fairly sure of the answer, Apple asked, "You didn't give her anything, did you?"

"Nothing to give."

"Except, of course, the answers to the questions she's just been asking you."

"Yes."

"About the missing item."

"Right," Harry said.

"You didn't throw it away," Apple stated, "so you must've burned it."

"No, I didn't."

"Oh? You mean you kept it?"

"No, I didn't do that."

Peevishly, Apple said, "If you didn't throw it away and you didn't destroy it and you didn't keep it, what else could you do with it?"

Harry droned tiredly, "I ate it."

"You did what?"

"I ate it," the conjurer said. "The item was a corned-beef sandwich."

EPILOGUE

Apple left the United Kingdom Philological Institute promptly at five o'clock in the afternoon. That allowed him ample time to stroll to the rendezvous point.

This was Apple's first day back at work. He had been at his cottage over the past days, having gone there after returning to Percy's Club its performer, who had insisted that the show must go on. Apple had felt that the second part of the Great Harold's engagement wouldn't run quite as smoothly as the first.

During the journey to his country home, Apple had stopped only once: to call in and tell the answering voice the nature of the famous item.

At the cottage Apple had rested from his efforts, nursed his aches and pains (with affection, recalling causation), enjoyed Monico's silent company, ignored his spy novel and not thought about Sylvia.

Apple had additionally done a little wrap-up paperwork. The result of this, two letters, he had mailed in the nearby village to box numbers in London.

Letter one was to Accounts. Apple sent in an itemised bill showing that he had spent the exact sum of forty-one pounds, not a penny more or less, including the price of two stamps. The bill had been difficult to work out. At last, rather than exaggerate the estimated expenses, such as petrol, Apple had bought a bouquet of red roses. They rested now in the silver vase on Ethel's dashboard.

Letter two, to Angus Watkin, was an operation report. In it Apple explained why he hadn't stayed out of the mission's last phase, the tracing of the pertinent pickpocket: Sylvia herself having found a clue, he had been forced to stick with her in order to try to get the man first; and sticking with Sylvia is what he had been ordered to do anyway.

Apple did not, however, offer in his letter any explanation for taking Harry away by force from the motorcycle Brits. He merely suggested that this matter should not be put into a written report.

Apple whistled as he strolled. He knew he was not going to get a rocket from Angus Watkin.

At five-fifteen Apple arrived at the specified corner on Cromwell Road. One minute later a grey car drew into the kerb and stopped. The driver was Albert. Sole passenger, in the back, was Angus Watkin.

After exchanging a sardonic glance with Albert, Apple opened the rear door and got in. "Good afternoon, sir," he said, settling on the seat.

"Porter," Angus Watkin acknowledged, almost with a hint of surprise, as though he himself had not instigated this rendezvous by telephoning his underling at work an hour ago, or as though he had doubted said underling's ability not only to find the place but to be there on time.

When Albert had steered the car back into the sluggish traffic, and when a panel of glass had risen smoothly to divide the interior, Angus Watkin said, "I got your report. It was more or less as expected."

"Thank you, sir," Apple said, as if in answer to praise. "I also called in to identify the mystery item."

"You were a little late with that," Angus Watkin said. "At the club, Harry was telling all and sundry of this fuss about a sandwich."

"But he didn't know what it meant."

"Do you, Porter? In espionage terms?"

"Well, nothing, sir, of course. The value must've been in the wrapping paper, which Harry burned."

Angus Watkin shook his head. "No, the paper wouldn't count. It could have been what Narkov intended doing with the sandwich itself that gave out information. How many bites he took, in what type of place he discarded it. That kind of thing."

"Or," Apple suggested, "the whole deal could have been a Red's herring for us while they were up to something else."

"Or the sandwich was a message to *him*. Corned beef could have meant that his game was up."

"Whatever his game might have been," Apple said by way of asking a question.

Not obliging, Angus Watkin said, "But let us get to your report. One detail was absent. Hence this meeting."

"Perhaps, sir, you refer to the men on a motor bike."

"Pray do not be facetious. Of course I mean that pair. Please explain your actions, Porter."

Cautioning himself not to be too glib, Apple began, "As you know, there's a story circulating in the underworld, a mixture of fact and fiction, that a protection-racket gang is moving in on the pickpockets of London, spreading fear so that there'll be no resistance when the collection of dues starts later."

Angus Watkin asked, "And?"

"And I had to save Harry to maintain his faith in me. He believed that the gang was on to him."

"Why would he believe that?"

Apple said, "Because this rumour has it that the gang uses goons on motor bikes, two sharing a machine, to chase down the dips and damage their working hands."

Apple tried not to make too much show of slowly flexing his right hand. He did it for only a moment, while looking out of the window and listening to the silence, which Angus Watkin broke with, "Tell me, Porter, why you could not have put that in your report."

"I didn't want to get the motor-bike pair into trouble with Upstairs," Apple said.

"Trouble, Porter?"

"It was a bad mistake on their part, coming on the scene in the very manner that had started that rumour in the first place."

Since, as Apple knew, the pair of faceless ones would never act of their own volition in a caper, the order to move in at Percy's could only have come from the man in charge of the operation—Angus Watkin.

Who was creating silence again.

Apple didn't know if it meant rage at the possible insult, disbelief that one might have been given, shock at having made a tactical error, or confusion over the he-knows and I-knows.

Seeing with a glance aside that his Control looked as normal, semi-lifeless, Apple thought that perhaps the error was his own. Maybe the motor-cycle duo were not faceless ones. As full agents, they wouldn't have waited for orders.

In which case, Apple wondered, would Angus Watkin appreciate the underling's assumed kindness in keeping the pair's mistake out of the written report, or would he condemn his lack of professionalism for not putting it in?

Apple was feeling confused himself. But he thought that whichever/whatever, he was safe from censure and a Watkin revenge for the big wrong—his interference.

Again Angus Watkin was the one to break the silence. He said, astonishingly, "I am going to tell you a joke."

Apple turned to stare worriedly at his chief. "Did you say a joke, sir?"

"I did, Porter."

"About the motor-bike pair?"

"No. You have explained. That closes the matter. I shall now recount a joke which is, apparently, funny, though I confess I have never been able to see the humour in it."

With his Control back in character, Apple relaxed. He listened as Watkin went on to tell of a workman who left the factory every night with his wheelbarrow. Suspecting theft, guards at the gate questioned him regularly as well as making spot checks of his clothes and the wheelbarrow's every part.

"Convinced now of theft," Angus Watkin said, "the guards offered the workman immunity from prosecution if, to ease their minds, he would tell them what he had been stealing. He agreed. And what, Porter, did he say?"

Promptly, Apple answered, "Wheelbarrows."

His Control nodded. "Correct, Porter. A psychological anecdote which some see as a joke. It is apropos to the Narkov affair."

"It is, sir?"

"Yes, Porter, entirely. We were all ignoring the obvious. We were all taking great note of everything that Narkov did on his afternoons off, down to the last detail. In the restaurants and similar places we paid super attention to the waiter, the type of food served, the nearby diners, the bill and money that changed hands, the time factor. Correct?"

"Yes, sir."

"What we did not bother to consider was that Narkov was *eating* those dishes."

Apple started to nod slowly. He said, "Narkov was on a strict diet."

"Exactly. And hated it. Therefore he began to break it when away from watch-dog wife and others at the embassy. He slipped around guiltily, arousing everyone's suspicion—in the wrong direction—while stuffing himself."

"On that last day," Apple said, "he went to a Chinese restaurant, an ice-cream parlour and a confectioner's."

Watkin said, "Devouring therein a large meal, an elaborate sundae and several Danish pastries."

"Probably on top of his usual lunch at home."

"Quite. He overdid it—and died."

"So the corned-beef sandwich was to be his final goody of the orgy."

"If," Angus Watkin said, "my interpretation is correct. I suspect it is. Can you think of a better, Porter?"

After a moment Apple said, "All I can think about right now is why Narkov was on the wrong platform at Piccadilly Station."

"I would suggest that, already feeling ill, he had become confused."

Apple nodded, still thinking. He noted that they were slowing to a halt near the office building on Regent Street.

When the car had stopped he said: "Perhaps Narkov had, after all, been collecting bits of information on his afternoons off. Perhaps, sure he would be followed, he acted in a guilty way to attract attention, and then let it be seen that it was only his diet he was cheating. A neat allayer that was just a bit too subtle. And perhaps the sandwich was so important that he had to get it somewhere fast, change train direction."

"And as a final perhaps," Angus Watkin said, "he had a heart attack on discovering that the sandwich was missing."

Apple said, "Right."

Watkin opened the door. "Not bad, Porter, but I prefer my own interpretation." He glanced out, towards the building, as if hesitating.

Apple had the impression that his chief was wondering if, by way of reward for work on the caper, he should invite his underling in. Apple cleared his throat companionably.

Angus Watkin got out. "Come along, Porter," he said. "Some female recruits are here to see films taken during the Narkov operation. You should find one of these particularly interesting. We found it when checking over the Earl's Court flat that Sylvia hastily vacated."